"Bittersweet, poignant, dist... milestone in Southern story...

—*Lambda Book Report*

"EXTRAORDINARY . . . reads like a beautiful and disturbing dream—but its power comes from the dream's truth, arresting and holding us to the end."

—Josephine Humphreys,
author of *Fireman's Fair*

"No one among the current crop of gay authors writes quite like Greene. He is a true Southern writer with a very distinctive style—a lyric romanticism aided by fine, often striking metaphors."

—George Stambolian,
editor of the *Men on Men* anthologies

"Imagine the limpidity of Tennessee Williams' short stories wed to the outsider friendships of a Capote or McCullers novel. Imagine the story at hand is still about youth, sex, and love, and you've got this effortlessly readable novel. . . . A terrifically sad and lovely piece of work."   —*Booklist*

HARLAN GREENE is the author of the highly acclaimed *Why We Never Danced the Charleston*. He lives in Chapel Hill, North Carolina.

HARLAN GREENE

WHAT THE DEAD REMEMBER

Withdrawn

A PLUME BOOK

PLUME
Published by the Penguin Group
Penguin Books USA Inc., 375 Hudson Street, New York, New York 10014, U.S.A.
Penguin Books Ltd, 27 Wrights Lane, London W8 5TZ, England
Penguin Books Australia Ltd, Ringwood, Victoria, Australia
Penguin Books Canada Ltd, 10 Alcorn Avenue, Toronto, Ontario, Canada M4V 3B2
Penguin Books (N.Z.) Ltd, 182-190 Wairau Road, Auckland 10, New Zealand

Penguin Books Ltd, Registered Offices: Harmondsworth, Middlesex, England

Published by Plume, an imprint of New American Library, a division of Penguin Books USA Inc.
Previously published in a Dutton edition.

First Plume Printing, December, 1992
10 9 8 7 6 5 4 3 2 1

REGISTERED TRADEMARK—MARCA REGISTRADA

LIBRARY OF CONGRESS CATALOGING-IN-PUBLICATION DATA
Greene, Harlan.
    What the dead remember / Harlan Greene.
        p.   cm.
    ISBN 0-452-26865-6
    I. Title.
    [PS3557.R3799W48   1991b]
    813'.54—dc20   92–53575
                                                            CIP

Printed in the United States of America
Original hardcover designed by Steven N. Stathakis

PUBLISHER'S NOTE:
This is a work of fiction. Names, characters, places, and incidents either are the product of the author's imagination or are used fictitiously, and any resemblance to actual persons, living or dead, events, or locales is entirely coincidental.

BOOKS ARE AVAILABLE AT QUANTITY DISCOUNTS WHEN USED TO PROMOTE PRODUCTS OR SERVICES.
FOR INFORMATION PLEASE WRITE TO PREMIUM MARKETING DIVISION, PENGUIN BOOKS USA INC.,
375 HUDSON STREET, NEW YORK, NEW YORK 10014.

For Olin
For Ever

CHARLESTON

Calm as that second summer which precedes
　　The first fall of the snow
In the broad sunlight of heroic deeds,
　　The City bides the foe.

As yet, behind their ramparts stern and proud,
　　Her bolted thunders sleep—
Dark Sumter, like a battlemented cloud,
　　Looms o'er the solemn deep.
　　　. . . . .
Thus girt without and garrisoned at home,
　　Day patient following day,
Old Charleston looks from roof, and spire, and dome,
　　Across her tranquil bay.
　　　. . . . .
Shall the Spring dawn, and she still clad in smiles,
　　And with an unscathed brow,
Rest in the strong arms of her palm-crowned isles,
　　As fair and free as now?

We know not; in the Temple of the Fates
　　God has inscribed her doom;
And all untroubled in her faith, she waits
　　The triumph or the tomb.

　　　　　　　　　—HENRY TIMROD, 1863

PART

1

PAROQUET

IT BEGAN THAT SUMMER I first saw the sea. I was thirteen. A big black taxi, as long as a hearse, picked me up at the Charleston airport and took me to that strange old house behind high walls surrounded by trees. I stopped when I saw Aunt Violet and Uncle Reynaldo. Grim as figures in a soot-blackened painting, they reached out and took me with them behind the screen.

After that, no one came but the mailman. Every day I went out on the porch and waited as if on a ship: one sunk in summer, stagnant and green. Vines laced everything, swelling over poles so they looked like green dinosaurs lifting their heads over the city. At noon, sirens rippled from across the water that I could sense but not see, and every now and then there were closer cracks and shudders; the earth shook beneath my feet.

I was lost. Poppa was back home in Illinois, and postcards from Momma and Francine came from faraway places in England, France, and Germany. Great-aunt Violet and Great-uncle Reynaldo did not talk much; they just looked at one another and shook their heads. I wanted them to speak, for I needed to know what the sounds were, and what to call those trees with the restless fronds whose brushings on one another, like an itch, irked me. I needed to know what was going on inside me.

All I was aware of that summer was me—I was hot, I was scared, I was cranky. I had no idea what was beginning. But one day as the ground shook, I ran to the front door like a drowning man reaching for the surface of the water. I flung my arms out wide, wanting to shout, "Save me!"

But like Aunt Violet and Uncle Reynaldo, I did not say a thing.

And so, these afternoons under the trees, when I think about that summer, it comes up as silently as an old black-and-white movie. The houses rise up, unreal, deserted, and open, gaping in grief.

The whole place was of ancient, outmoded things. When sounds came, they too were ghost songs issued from Aunt Violet's radio, and I expected last year's shows to appear on their television. The houses, with their blank windows, made the buildings seem not so much asleep as dazed and dreaming, dozing in heat. With only the white shades showing, they looked like eyes rolled up in a trance, like a swami's.

One afternoon when I had been with them about a week, Aunt Violet and I went shopping. I pushed the groceries in the squeaky old cart with the bent wheel, remembering what Uncle Reynaldo had told me. Moving like snails, we left trails on the sweating concrete. Mirages rose sky-high, and time was slowed by the heat.

Uncle Reynaldo had told me about the Civil War,

which had begun in Charleston, he said, over slavery. He told me about the dreadful things that had happened in the city. He pointed out where slaves had been sold, where they had been imprisoned, poisoned, and where they had been hanged for conspiring. There were so many points. Everywhere we went, the past rose around us. History rumbled like thunder in the distance and worked up from underneath, like tree roots splitting the concrete. Aunt Violet and I turned down a street, and a cool, damp blast shot from a grille under a building.

I knew it was the stale exhalation of time, the breath of centuries.

We stopped by a cemetery; Aunt Violet went in. I wouldn't because I thought I could hear the dead speaking.

> *This is what happened to us.*
> *(There were so many of us once.)*
> *This is what happened to me.*

At night I read in bed, and when I fell asleep I had vivid technicolor dreams that broke into my consciousness as violently as storms, or storm troopers did in movies. I woke feeling strange as if I had been on the verge of breaking through to some revelation. I cocked my ear as if I could hear singing. But the feeling disappeared, like something receding underwater, only to haunt and linger and taunt me.

That next morning I lay in bed blinking as the sunlight came in sticky and yolk yellow. I heard Aunt Violet and Uncle Reynaldo. Downstairs, the refrigerator door clasped and unclasped, drawers grated, silver rattled against plates.

When I came down, they looked at each other with the same surprised, rabbit-like blinks. But they did not say a thing.

———

It was that way every morning. I ate my eggs and toast and drank watered-down coffee, and Aunt Violet compared me to those pathetic yellow and brown boys she and Reynaldo read of in her magazines.

Sometimes she was prompted to speak.

"You're not the only boy in the world who's ever been unhappy," she once told me.

"No, ma'am," I agreed.

They were like figures from a nursery rhyme, or an allegory, as important to each other as air is to breathing. Aunt Violet and Uncle Reynaldo had been married for over fifty years. Soon after their wedding, however, they had left Charleston for Rangoon, Jakarta, and New Delhi. Retired missionaries, they had returned to the city and called for me.

Uncle Reynaldo was short and fine, while Aunt Violet was tall and thin, and as awkward and gawky as their parrot that stayed mostly on its ring. She had cropped gray hair, slightly crossed eyes, and snaggle teeth. Every day she rose out of the stairwell, like something from a trapdoor, to wake me.

But she was a woman, so I took to her first. Women, I found, were more apt to be nice to me. Uncle Reynaldo was slower to speak; he just looked sadly back over his shoulder as he went down the hall after breakfast to his library. Later, when I started to follow him, he looked like one of the sand or ghost crabs I'd see scuttling down the beach.

He'd beckon, but when I tried to follow him, Aunt Violet would loom in the doorway and stand in the dark hall with her arms folded across her chest like a genie. She'd march me back to the sink and hand over the dish towel.

One morning when the dishes were done, she told me to go out and play in the overgrown yard. Lying out in the grass like snakes were rusty metal things. She insisted.

So I went out to the stoop with my head down, sure she was being mean—for I was certain Momma must have taken her aside and told her about me.

Back home, everybody knew. I was never chosen for teams; Francine rolled her eyes and said, "Momma, make him stop!" as I followed her around in the evenings; Poppa had long since stopped throwing me footballs in the field. It was best to just let me be.

But not Aunt Violet. She said she knew all about boys, how we should be.

"Then why didn't you ever have one?" I wanted to say. I wanted to stay inside and read or follow Reynaldo into his library, but Aunt Violet did not allow it.

"Out you go," she said, and pointed at the door.

To her, we were like dogs. Boys should come inside only to eat and to sleep.

If Lula the maid was there, I looked to her for help.

One morning Lula looked up from that iron she was passing back and forth over sheets as if doomed, like Sisyphus, to move it eternally. She sighed, and the whites of her eyes gleamed.

I went outside, careful not to slam the screen, and I sat on the back steps listening to the thump of the iron behind me, idly watching the lizards play like tiny dinosaurs in the ivy. Over the wall were the city's steeples and trees.

I turned back and listened to Aunt Violet trying to trick Lula.

"Call me Vi," she said.

But Lula was wary.

Speaking to the other colored ladies at the bus stop that afternoon, Lula complained that Aunt Violet was trying to trap her in trouble. "She always wantin' me to come in the *front* door," Lula said, "trying to get me to join the N-double-A-C-P."

When she told this to the others, they shook their heads and sucked their gold-rimmed teeth as they did over a sick baby.

"Crazy times comin'," they said, and looked down the street as if it were that and not the bus they were expecting to see.

Lula answered Aunt Violet with a "Yes, ma'am" or a "No, ma'am," and because it was not what Violet wanted, it made me feel that Lula and I were in league.

All that day long and on the ones following, I sat listening, waiting for the sounds to change. When they did, I peered in through the screen.

One day the coast was clear: I stole in through the kitchen to the hall. Lula turned her eyes on me.

I pleaded with her mutely, but she did something odd.

She cleared her throat loudly. Aunt Violet jerked awake: she woke blinking and then focused on me.

"Out!" she screamed.

Lula smiled. I went back outside, the screen door like a slap on my fanny.

I waited, and one day soon after I caught Lula eating ice cream. Aunt Violet was always trying to bribe her with it, saying, "Come on, have some." Lula would make a face and answer, "No, ma'am, that cold stuff doan agree with me."

But she was eating it right out of the carton with a rice spoon. The strawberry was as pink and startling as the tongue in her dark face when she stuck it out at me.

"Lula," I whispered from outside the screen. "Look!"

She froze as I came in the door, waiting to see what I would do.

I paused by Aunt Violet and looked down on her.

She was asleep in her rocker, head thrown back and arms dangling. Her Bible was open in her lap, its thin pages flipping back and forth as if some invisible hand (the Holy Ghost's?) was in search of something.

I reached over to wake her. Lula looked venomously at me.

"Ha, ha!" I whispered.

I left them in the kitchen and slipped down the dark hall to the library.

Of all the rooms in that bracketed, old house—the attic, the twisted back steps piled high with *National Geographics*, and the room with bars on the window and a dressmaker's dummy, it is the library that first comes back to me. It had red-flocked wallpaper, was damp, and inside the bay window I could peep out through the slats of the shutters to the street.

I sneaked in and stared at the dark, varnished shelves and the Gothic-arched doors. Inside were shadow boxes of Reynaldo's mounted moths and butterflies. All around were statues (one of a monkey with a human skull in its hand, regarding it sadly), fossils, and funny-shaped brass rings. What interested me the most, however, was a bird under a glass dome that Uncle Reynaldo said was extinct.

I repeated the word as I approached, saying *extinct* like *date*. Or *prom*. Or *acne*. They were some of the blond words I overheard my sister, Francine, use. When I said them, I shivered and my head spun, like eating ice cream too quickly.

Extinct did not seem possible, for the bird looked real. I crept up on my knees so it would not see me. I rose up slowly.

Sitting on the branch was a redheaded yellow-and-green bird called a Carolina Paroquet. There had been thousands of them once. So many, in fact, that the Indians (who were gone, too) had spoken of talking trees. They had been everywhere. Uncle Reynaldo told me he had seen one of the last ones in the wild—in a tree on Sullivan's Island in the summer of 1912 or '13.

Maybe it was because I was as lonely as it must have been, was why I drawn to it. Or maybe it was something else.

Holding my breath, I raised my head up slowly in the hope of catching it ruffling its feathers, blinking an eye, preening.

"Boo!" I cried, but not a sound, not a peep, came from the Carolina Paroquet.

As I stood in front of it, a claw reached from behind. I almost screamed. I turned around and saw Uncle Reynaldo grinning at me. He brought me closer and pointed out its features.

"I saw it die," he whispered. His glasses fogged; his breath was bad, like the gasps from cellars under buildings. He said his mate had died, and the bird stayed next to her, mourning. Then he turned his great, lens-magnified eyes my way as if gauging the effect it had on me.

After that, I gave the paroquet a wide berth, but I still sneaked into Reynaldo's library. The books, like specimens behind the glass doors, kept pulling me. Every time in, I opened a door and took down a book; I held it as delicately as if it were a bird—opening its boards was spreading its wings. They smelled old and musty and were magic, for they stored time the way the house stored heat. To release it, like the house did heat in the evenings, rising up like hosannahs, all I had to do was flip through the pages and read.

Then not only did the stories rise up, but the sense of those others who had turned the pages before came, too. If a folded leaf, or a pressed blossom, fell out, then the time when it had been picked and pressed was revealed. Visions of other summers, of other people I had not known, glimmered like light on water. Tumbled views of green meadows and ladies in long white dresses with puffed sleeves fanned out. There was a young boy with a net chasing butterflies; and yellow and green birds in trees. Vista after vista opened up. I read *Ivanhoe, Robinson Crusoe* and *David Copperfield*.

But then there always came a sound, when Aunt Violet woke or Lula came in. I'd have to put the book down quickly and gasp, looking around the damp, close room like someone lost, looking at the engravings on the walls from Shakespeare—*The Merchant of Venice, Othello, Twelfth Night*, all foxed badly—and at Reynaldo's many degrees. I came to and scrambled out quickly, as sometimes Uncle Reynaldo, risen from his afternoon nap, appeared.

He was a fine, hunched little man who was always folding in on himself like origami. He was as fragile as the little Chinese figurine in our hall back home—so white it was almost blue with its tiny, fine hand stroking its long mandarin beard.

The light that came through the speckled shades was yellow and dingy, so Uncle Reynaldo always used a magnifying glass with a spotlight built in to read. If he beckoned, I'd go over to plug it in for him. He would sit with his shadow boxes of butterflies piled on his knees, so that his own shadow would flutter its wings teasingly above him on the ceiling.

I'd sit on the frizzy old carpet at his feet and peer at what he had in his hand. Once he opened his palm to reveal a fine old ring; another time he showed me a soft white tuft of something that looked like cotton and smiled a huge grin, empty of teeth.

He brought his hand to my eye and looked back and forth. Then he blew on the tuft and, like a dandelion, it fell softly. It was a tuft of his own hair, and it seemed to fall like snow, taking years to reach the carpet. When it hit, he looked at me as if asking if I thought it was funny.

But I kept going back to the library, drawn by something. I would often hear him talking, and since there was no one else in there, I peered around the doorjamb wondering if Uncle Reynaldo could see into the netherworld, like I could see down into the world underwater if I peered closely. But it was to himself he was speaking.

As he spoke, he grew excited. Often I'd see him holding an insect up to the light like a jewel of great price, saying, "Yes, yes, yes."

He'd close his eyes as if in a trance and he'd dredge its name up from memory.

Then the thing in his hand would shiver and I would, too. I was dragged from behind the door and over to Reynaldo's chair, just like a moth dragged against screens at night.

I came up as he drew out the long Latin name as rapturously as a priest, and in that name lay not just a designation but a destiny.

I wanted that, too.

I wanted to be named, to be claimed. I wanted to know what those feelings were that plagued me. I thought all words were as magic as *thank you* or *please*. Like apologies, like love, I thought words had the power to heal. The nameless things I did during the day held no substance until I told them to someone else. But with no one to talk to that summer, I was a ghost. I wanted something real to happen to me.

We established an unvarying routine. Every day at noon, Lula brought in plates of tomato sandwiches and salads of green peas and cheese—we ate at a white enamel table in the cool, dim pantry. After she took the dishes away, Aunt Violet and Uncle Reynaldo went upstairs for their naps. I pictured them upside down in the attic, hanging like bats in their wings.

The downstairs changed to Lula's then as she changed

the music on the radio, careful to turn it back from the colored station before leaving. Trombones wailed, jazz stretched, and sometimes people sang moodily. It made me uneasy. She invited other maids over from the houses up the street. While Uncle Reynaldo and Aunt Violet slept, they watched their "stories" on TV. Sometimes Lula was alone, and I often ran into her in the library with an old apothecary jar or something else in her hand, looking down into it as if it were a tunnel and she too was looking for a way out of summer.

She always stopped when she saw me.

"Go on, white boy," she said. "You know your aunt ain't allow you in here."

I'd go out and sit on the porch for a while, wondering why she did not like me.

One day, I opened the gate and peered out. Summer seemed like a desert I was fated to cross until fall came to release me.

I wandered the streets, slowly at first, then more and more quickly, for I sensed something beyond touch, just beyond reach. It was like the ice cream truck, its nursery rhymes magnified. I kept after it, turning corner after corner. I could see it in the distance, but it was something I could never reach.

One day, however, I thought I made it through. I came up to a little blond boy. He blinked as if he had just touched down from another sphere.

"Hello," he said and held out his hand. "I'm Peyton."

I confessed my name and he looked at me as if to say he was sorry. But he got an idea. He motioned me toward an overgrown fence.

I watched as he picked honeysuckle. Very delicately he withdrew the stamen and curled his tongue and licked the sweet drop of dew from the bottom of it. Then he folded the blossom and put it down like discarding a nasty cocktail napkin at a party.

"Want to come?"

I nodded. He pulled back the vines on the fence, like drawing back drapes, and showed me a hole in a chain-link fence. I was in awe, for it was just what I had always believed: another world, the one of my dreams, existed parallel to my own, waiting for me. We crawled through the hole in the fence into a playground I had never seen. He ran over to the merry-go-round and demanded that I push him.

"Faster, faster!" he screamed. He pretended he was riding a horse and with his make-believe whip, he lashed at me.

I pushed faster. I whinnied.

He got off the merry-go-round and stood there while I sat on the ground.

"I'm famous," he said, twirling.

In a high child's voice Peyton told me that he had lit the fuse of the cannon that the United Daughters of the Confederacy had fired on the one hundredth anniversary of the start of the War Between the States in a big ceremony. "We're going to win it this time!"

A color picture of Peyton had appeared in the "These Women!" section of the paper one Sunday.

"Are you a Yankee?" he asked as we sat down under some trees.

I told him that I did not know.

"Then you must be!" he said.

His pale blue eyes, the color of the stripes in his seersucker shorts, took on light.

"Look at that!" he shouted and pointed to the air. "A spaceship!"

I looked over the trees at the sky that revealed nothing other than a long white cloud. It pointed at the horizon like a skeletal finger.

"I don't see anything."

When I looked back, he was gone. I ran over to the fence and thought I could hear the fabric swishing from the other side as he ran.

"Stop!" I called out. "Peyton!"

But he was not in the street.

I hoped he would be back in the playground the next day, but there were only some colored boys on the jungle gym; they dropped off and walked away, watching me, and crept back after I left.

I searched for Peyton for weeks—in the park and the streets; but I never saw him again. It was worse than if he had never appeared, for I knew the other world was true.

It existed for others, but not for me.

A few times I saw other boys off in the distance; they ran away when I chased them. Wanting them to like me, I closed my eyes, and concentrated, *I'll do anything*.

But they did not receive my message. When they turned my way at all it was just to sniff at me suspiciously, like dogs. Somehow they knew my status—as if it were stamped on my forehead.

"Fatso," they called. "Four-eyes" or "Sissy."

Like a bull, I ran after them and they scattered.

They looked back at me as if I was a prehistoric beast crawling out of the ocean to destroy Tokyo in one of those awful afternoon science-fiction movies.

I ran after them, and a raw horror of disgust and unhappiness welled up in me as I made ugly faces and shouted terrible things.

They just danced away and dodged like matadors, singing, "Can't catch me! Can't catch me!"

"I'll show you," I screamed.

At home, when I came in crying, Momma patted me

and said, "Don't worry, it'll be all right." But when I came back to Aunt Violet's, she and Uncle Reynaldo were still upstairs asleep. Lula was serving her friends goodies that Violet had taught her to make; they curled up their pinkies and laughed, mimicking the old white ladies.

I lingered in the hallway.

But, "Go on," Lula said, "look like you got *too* much to eat."

I went into the kitchen, shoveled out a huge bowl of ice cream, and took the book I had found in Reynaldo's library.

The book was about a boy who had no one else, so he made friends with the ghosts that haunted the old house next to his family's. They taught him things and helped him play tricks on kids who had treated him cruelly.

It was called *Ghost Summer*; and I read it continually.

Coming home one afternoon, I took a wrong turn and ended up in a part of town off King Street. Tremors came from a huge crane that loomed high over the tops of buildings.

It gained momentum in a swing.

I pressed through the crowd and saw a row of columns, and a row of people watching. The columns were two stories high and Greek. When the ball hit one, it toppled into another, dissolving instantly, like sugar in tea. Dust rose up like a roar or a cheer.

"Oh!" I thought. I danced like Peyton.

I knew if they were awake, Aunt Violet and Uncle Reynaldo would be looking at each other and shaking their heads. I now knew why the earth shook: bulldozers were tearing down part of the old city. There was a pit down into which I could peer.

Looking in, I imagined the boys in the crater. I pictured them naked, tied to sticks of dynamite, and I had the plunger in my hand. As they lay there, they kicked and screamed and pleaded:

"Save me! Please! I'm sorry!"

It made me happy and set up a magic tingling, like touching a secret place, in me.

When I got home, the skies were streaked with evening. Lula was gone.

"Where have you been?" Aunt Violet asked.

When I told her, she was upset.

"They're tearing down everything," she said in a querulous old voice. "Don't you go back there."

I assured her I wouldn't, and felt wicked as I found my way back there the next morning.

I loved it. It was like walking on the moon or through a war-torn landscape from the movies. The sky shone through roofless walls; trucks rode up on sidewalks; people came out of buildings carrying old doors, like stretchers. They brought out mantels and shutters and even chandeliers. Every now and then the whistle would blow again; the wrecking ball would swing.

I'm destroying it, I'd pretend as it flew through the air. *It's me*. The crash and clatter delighted me.

I'd go home along King Street, sometimes stopping to buy candy. One day I saw a building I had never noticed before. I stood in front of the drugstore and blinked. It had been modernized; but looming up behind its sleek facade was the building's original Victorian trappings; the rounded upstairs windows looked like spying eyes. I pressed my face to the plate glass so I could see. There were magazines.

I went in. It was air-conditioned, and summer dissolved instantly.

I moved as if in a dream, passing shelves of soap and colognes, wrapped in the smell of eucalyptus and the quiver of fluorescent lighting.

The women working in the aisles were as silent as nuns, as efficient as nurses in their white uniforms and crackling white stockings. I floated by—past cardboard cutouts of carts with red-and-white-striped awnings that looked like props from *An American in Paris*. The air conditioning was lulling; so was the cool, white, guileless hygiene.

I stopped, heart thudding, in front of the magazines. I looked around. At my last checkup back home, the dentist had caught me.

"I won't tell your mother," he said, looking over his glasses and pulling the torn sheet from my hand. But he did not use Novocain; the thrill and the drill filling my cavities were all mixed up with the magazines.

I was scared and started sweating. My hands were so wet I had to wipe them on my jeans. I picked up a copy of the *Saturday Evening Post*, but then hurled it down and picked up a boy magazine, a *Popular Mechanics* or a *Field and Stream*, when a lady came up to get a *Good Housekeeping*. She nodded her little winged hat at me and left.

Then I picked up the *Saturday Evening Post* again.

I looked around.

I glanced up into one of those rounded mirrors suspended from the corner of the ceiling and saw myself: a distorted little thing. I took a deep breath.

I turned the page and stopped. There they were: complete, requiring no imagination; as full-blown as images on television. I breathed out, transfixed at what I saw, but it was more like a space within me, really. I saw a black-and-white picture of men and boys advertising Hanes or BVDs.

It was as if I had come upon them secretly, like one would a deer in woods, or birds on the edge of a marsh, unaware anyone was watching. They seemed so near. The poignancy of their beauty almost brought me to tears.

I had money. But it felt so illicit, like the boy with the ghosts in the book, that I sensed the woman at the cash register would not sell me the magazine. So I had to steal. I folded the page back and tore slowly; it was worse than trying to open a crinkly piece of candy in church.

When it was done, I looked around. The world had not ended. The druggist was still behind his high blond wood counter; the ladies were still moving efficiently.

Shaking, I put the magazine down and stuffed the ad in my pocket. I broke into a run and the little Greek lady behind the cash register swiveled around as I burst out blindly into the street, where it was too hot to breathe, too bright to see.

"Hey!"

I jumped.

But it was just some boys on the corner.

"You," they shouted, "come here."

I shook my head and walked on. I no longer needed them. I made the same face at them that kids back home made at retarded Otis Farrabee.

They started to chase me. As I ran, I made my plans. I'd go up the creaky old steps as quickly as spawning salmon going upstream. I'd lock my door, lower the shades, and take my clothes off. It would be like water on flames, relief, as I lay naked in front of the piece from the magazine.

But the front door was stuck; it banged against the wall as I rushed in.

"Boy!" Uncle Reynaldo called out.

I stopped. He held out the plug to his magnifier.

"Could you hook this thing in for me?"

Bending, I wondered if he could hear the crinkling of the paper in my pocket.

Next came Aunt Violet.

"Is that you?" she wanted to know as I approached the stairs.

"Yes, ma'am."

I started up and looked down from the first landing, but all she did was bat at herself with a handkerchief, wipe her shiny forehead, and say, "Well, slow down. No need to hurry in *this* heat," saying it as if someday there might be heat to merit speed.

"Yes, ma'am," I answered.

Once in my room, I locked the door and pulled the paper out. I pressed and flattened it and pored over it as if it were an ancient piece of papyrus with holy writ on it.

Naked I lay in front of it; it was a balm—as if I had taken the cool from the drugstore with me.

I dreamed, and a tremor shook the city.

Summer was finally starting for me.

SUMMER CHANGED THEN. Though I wandered the streets, I no longer searched. I moved along, contented. I dreamed.

Sometimes a call would come when I was in bed, in the shower, or out in the hollow green streets. I could even be asleep, yet suddenly the boys and men in the magazine would resonate—like vibrations in a pipe organ—that melancholy, that ghostly—and I'd have to obey. Racing to them, I felt the way I did in thunderstorms, running out into the fields, breathing the ionized air as if it were sweet.

A buoyancy, a weightless joy, would well up. And as I lay in front of them, my chin in my hands, they rose from the shiny magazine and led me urgently—madly—upward until I hovered; then we went over the edge, with no possible stopping.

The day went away then.

When it came back I was spent and different. Grateful

for the sensations they had brought, I had a moment of peace. But then the world returned, worse than it had been before, darker for the light that had just flashed through me. It was centered on my damp belly, bringing back the heat and shame and fear.

The boys were there. Impartial and imperial, they stood with their arms across their chests in a ring, oblivious in their maleness and BVDs.

I had to cringe from them, facedown, to the bathroom. When I returned, I had to put them away quickly.

But I always went back, to regain that magic moment outside time, to regain peace. In the Sahara of that summer, they were my only oases. They were like evenings—when the earth turned away from the sun and we heaved a sigh of relief.

Summer evenings in Charleston were like passages— not just between day and night, but between day and dreams, the crash of Scylla and Charybdis. In that slanted, triumphant light, shutters opened, birds sang, and people appeared on balconies. It was possible to believe.

The boys and evening brought on dreams. It was a mystical feeling, the yearning the creative must feel or the dumb know wanting to speak. I wanted to be with the men and boys in the pictures and be them simultaneously. They brought out a new part of me; and everyone else was transcending, too. Aunt Violet and Uncle Reynaldo appeared downstairs like music box figurines, blinking like fish flooded back to life after lying in a dried stream. They looked about in the dusk, their eyes wide and mouths gaping as if they had come out of a coma, and the day already was far away: a dim and imperfect memory.

Poplars along the street turned their leaves to silver and shimmered like discs on tambourines as I lay in front of the magazine. The dying afternoon sunlight hit my flesh and burned like glory.

"Yes," I thought, feeling I could make it to where they called me.

Again and again I did it for the magic of believing. But every time it happened, the feeling, like dreams, disappeared.

When Lula left in the evening, she turned on the yellow bug light on the porch. That was the signal for evenings to end, and for night to come down like a wet woolen blanket: heavy, damp, and scratchy.

Downstairs we ate scrambled eggs on toast, sardines on saltines. Then we went back to our rooms to sleep.

The weeks passed, and summer was as shapeless and stretched out as the old T-shirts that hung off me.

The heat not only increased, it accumulated like dust under things. I paced for hours along the long, low side porch fringed with vines and overhung with leaves through which the light came through grotto-like and green.

Sometimes I lay down on my bed and looked at the ceiling. The cracks spread as I dreamed of the glass in the library cases shattering; I saw the house exploding, and all the books and butterflies rising up through a hole in the roof—the Carolina Paroquet and I would take wing.

Until then, I knew we were as doomed as figures on a bas relief: Aunt Violet, Uncle Reynaldo, and I would all be frozen effigies—she with her Bible in her lap in front of Lula, Uncle Reynaldo in the library, and me in my bed forever in front of the magazines. Nothing but fall could come to save us. But one day when the cycle seemed as fixed as the earth's orbit, Aunt Violet did something odd. She came into my room earlier than usual one morning and shook me awake. I rose but did not understand what was happening.

I looked out. Day was dawning. I saw Uncle Reynaldo in the yard pulling back the dark green doors to the old carriage house; it looked like a pterodactyl spreading its wings.

I ran down, and without a single look behind her, Aunt Violet backed the old DeSoto out to the street.

I grabbed up my things, as instructed, but then called out, "Wait!"

I ran back through the dark house and reached under the bed. I pulled out the pictures stolen from the magazines.

We rolled out of the city. The air was as vaporous and hazy as the smoke that billowed from the anthills I sometimes doused with kerosene: ants would come out running like the doomed when I lit the match.

"Where are we going?" I asked Uncle Reynaldo.

He turned and smiled but did not say a thing.

WE DROVE OVER THE BRIDGE
to the mainland. We passed the Dairy Queen and sailed
onto the causeway across the marshes to another bridge.
The first time I saw Sullivan's Island, it was low and flat,
its green subdued to muddy grays by the thick air, like a
mirage in the waving heat. I picked out backs of old forts,
a few white houses against the low trees, gables and towers
rising in peaks. To me it looked as fabulous as the cities
of domes and minarets I had glimpsed in *My Book of Bible
Stories*.

Uncle Reynaldo rode in the front seat with his head
out the window like a dog. When we got there, Aunt Violet
collapsed against the wheel as if she had landed a jet plane
singlehandedly.

Uncle Reynaldo got out first and opened her door,
then came over to my side and bowed low to me.

We had stopped at a tiny house far away down a

walkway. I followed Aunt Violet, who carried her bags high above the grass as if wading an alligator-infested stream. Crickets ceased their shrilling as she passed and then started up again; tricked, they stopped again for me.

The house leaned. Inside, I felt odd, as if we had left our selves back in the city; just as locusts leave their shells on the floor, molting, or as cripples leave their crutches when healed. Maybe we're still back there, I thought, and this is all a dream.

But I put my bags down. The house shook and I could see through the cracks to the soft dirt beneath.

Maybe we're poor, I thought, panicking, though my idea of poverty back then was living in an apartment instead of a house and not having a washing machine. It seemed possible, however: the house seemed as liable to tumble down as one of cards or a dandelion in a breeze. But it seemed a lark—like camping.

The beach house had one long central room bisected by an archway. On the left was a kitchen, a bathroom, and a pantry; on the right, a door to the hall between the two bedrooms—one for them and one for me. The paneling had once been painted and varnished in a mural of giant fishes, wrecks, and huge seaweed. In my room, there was only a bed, a chair, and a chest of drawers; the room was painted white halfway up the walls. There were spots on the gray-and-white mattress and stains on the ceiling.

I sat on the bed and the wire supports squeaked. I tugged the warped drawers of the chest open one side at a time to put my clothes in, and then concealed the pictures beneath. The boys looked up as panicked as if I were closing them into a coffin.

That whole day I helped clean while Uncle Reynaldo sat rocking on the front porch. I was afraid the people passing would look at the mattresses airing in the yard and assume that the one who had peed them was me.

But all around us people were doing the same thing. Like birds migrating, Charlestonians left their big downtown houses in June and came to their summer homes, where everything was worn and comfortable as Saturday clothing.

After supper Aunt Violet told me to go out to the front yard. She came down the steps.

"Come on, Rennie," she said, clapping her hands, as if calling a puppy.

He peered anxiously from the porch and inched down the steps one at a time.

Once on the ground, he clasped our hands and lifted them up and grinned, waving as if it were a huge victory.

As we went down the street into the darkening day, he held onto us as if afraid the wind might come up and raise him up like a kite. We turned down a pathway. There were dunes ahead, and a sense of something imminent. My heart beat as it had in the drugstore.

Back home I could stand on the back porch and see the fields of rippling corn and wheat on all sides, but as we topped the dunes and I saw the ocean, its size and restlessness amazed me. I stopped in awe, not knowing what to think.

In Sunday school I used to imagine Moses leading the children of Israel (I saw them as kindergartners) out of bondage, like a band leader up our street; and I pictured Ruth and Naomi in our fields. But this . . . this. I had nothing—no knowledge—to relate to the sea. It was a new world I was entering.

I did not understand why, in its restlessness, the sea did not dissolve the sand we were on, or what kept it from rushing up the drains, eroding the world, rising up to drown cities.

I stood atop the dune thrilled, wanting to dance and howl and scream. Aunt Violet went down into the light, which was as silvery as the water itself, and released her shawl; it billowed about her like smoke, but she pulled it in, to lie flat as a sleeve.

"Take your shoes off, boy," Uncle Reynaldo said, nudging me.

I slipped into the sand; it shifted and I jumped as if it were trying to eat me. But then I caught Uncle Reynaldo's crooked smile. I hurriedly got my socks off and carried them with my shoes as I went down to the edge. The water rose around me tantalizingly.

They walked on the shore; I paralleled them in the water. People passed, silent and mysterious as night birds. We went on walking. When we reached the bend of the island and I could go no farther without getting swept into the channel, we could see Charleston, could make out the white steeple of St. Michael's, the earthen gray of St. Philip's, and a few tall buildings. Fort Sumter was as big as Gibraltar in front of us, eclipsing the city.

The tide turned, going out to where the buoy lights blinked.

As it got darker, Charleston slipped away, as if we were on a liner putting out to sea. And when we turned to go back, we were facing the breeze.

Uncle Reynaldo pushed me toward the moon rising out of the water and said something about climbing up its rungs of light. I did not want to leave, but when we got back to the path they made me.

As I lay in bed, listening to the sea drowse, the shades blew in and out, matching the night's breath to mine and I thought of the boys in the magazine.

And then I remembered how when I had been younger, we used to go driving in my father's Plymouth, big and finned as a spaceship. We drove into the night and when we came back, Poppa carried me upstairs in his arms like Abraham carrying Isaac and Momma would come up to tuck me in and whisper, "Pleasant dreams."

A nostalgia for all I had believed in almost brought me to tears. It was the same feeling the boys brought me.

Sleeping that night was like being in the sea. I was lithe and buoyant, someone else entirely. And the feeling did not disappear when I woke the next morning.

I WENT TO THE BEACH. FOR days I lay in the water, as lazily as if in the arms of a lover, floating contentedly. It was ballet: I turned and spun acrobatically. I pretended I had friends. And one day they appeared.

What I saw far away in the haze was not on the sand; it was on the water, but it was not walking. It was long, black, and undulating like a snake toward me. I put my hand over my eyes to see better. Puzzled, I watched pieces of the thing break off and spin out separately. It looked like something out of Revelation or a movie.

The glare was so intense that I fell back. It neared, and still kept breaking into pieces of itself, wiggling off into small entities. The glare split open as if summer were a pod bursting to scatter seeds. Each rose up in definition almost simultaneously to reveal black spots like insects—they became bigger, real.

"Oh," I said out loud. I felt my knees wobbling.

There were six or seven boys, trim and brown and lean. They were near. Their burned skin peeled on their noses to show colors beneath.

They were lithe, they moved easily. Some were muscular, others as thin as those cardboard Halloween skeletons that dance in a breeze.

Each boy had a thin, round wafer of plywood that he threw out in front of him. As they threw and ran after them, leaping out and landing on the big boards with a splash, water flew around them and in a blur I could see the flash of their teeth. I danced as if they beckoned. They were smiling.

They skimmed along the shallows on those boards, striking poses against the light: with their arms flung out and their knees bent, they looked like oriental dancers in a frieze. They were so real, and hard to believe.

I laughed out loud and danced along after them, like a dog chasing birds. They nudged each other, looked at me, and I could not help smiling.

Then the siren wailed. I looked around to see if anyone else had noticed. The boys, however, ignored the sound that grew and grew like a crack or a scream. It was from the fire department—every day at noon they sounded it to make sure it would work in emergencies. Violet made it my signal to go home and eat.

While I was looking around, the boys went down the beach, as if in a conga line. The drops of water they flung out became spangling drops of light as they disappeared.

I was dazed and hollow in the afterglow, as empty as the indentations their feet made on the beach. Back home I opened up the drawer to see the black and white figures.

But something had happened to them; and to me.

———

At lunch I could barely eat. As if I had stared into the sun and looked away, the boys were all I could see. Everything else moved in a dim field.

I thanked Aunt Violet for lunch. She looked at me oddly.

"Are you all right?" she asked.

I nodded.

I wanted to go back, but Aunt Violet made me wait. "You'll cramp," she warned.

But I had already—with hope and with dreams. I checked the drawer again; they lay in there as if in a coffin. I felt pity for the pictures, and knew the boys would be waiting for me when I got back.

But the shore was blank, blazing. The sun, like fate or a sphinx, stared down at me. I kept twirling around, knowing that as soon as I turned my back, they would appear.

It could not *not* be. I wondered if I had imagined it, but I was so happy, it had to have been.

And was! I saw the boys off in the distance the next morning. Knowing that they were true, that we would eventually meet, was enough. I knew I had broken through, that my dreams were real.

And that afternoon when I climbed up to the dunes to look for the boys, something moved in the gully.

I started down, excited, but stopped. A strange, fat boy rose from the earth like something long buried: mud fell away, revealing his white, slug-like belly. His eyes attracted. They were wrong—like radium on my watch, less blue than green, aquamarine. They were too close together, leaving too much space in his round face.

His look changed from concentration to happiness when he saw me. He had been dredging mud from the bottom of the gully and pushing it up with his hands and packing it down along a dam he was building.

He was fat and shaped like a dumpling. His orange hair was cut straight across his face so that the bangs hung over his close-set eyes. He looked oriental with those fat cheeks.

"Retard," Francine would have said, dismissing him, and that made me think of Otis Farrabee back home. He didn't have all his marbles, folks said. Neither did the boy in front of me. When I asked him why he stared so, he smiled, and his freckles spilled unevenly across the bridge of his nose and cheeks. It gave his face a startled look that made me want to smile; I wanted to reach out and brush some of the dots off. I found myself staring at his frank face just as earnestly as he looked at me.

He looked so sweet and dumb and trusting.

"Hey," he said.

I was tempted to speak. But I remembered those glorious boys. They were somewhere nearby waiting for me, so I bit my lip. If I smiled the way he did, Francine would have said, "Wipe that idiotic look off your face."

Thinking of her made me dizzy, for I suddenly realized why she would have said that: she didn't like seeing me so happy.

The boy was like a magnet in how he disoriented me. But in my mother's best manner, I said, "Go away. You're weird." With my nose up in the air, I moved away regally.

He followed me up the beach, and when I looked back from the path, I was sort of disappointed that he did not follow me to the street.

That night, as usual, Aunt Violet asked me what I had done during the day. I told her about the boy, that he had thrown mud at me.

"You don't mean Stevie?" she asked skeptically.

As soon as she did, I knew I was in for it.

"He'd never be mean to anybody." She narrowed her eyes. "Did you start something?"

"No, ma'am!"

"Well, you must have," she theorized.

I listened as she told me wonderful things about Stevie. "He's kind, he's friendly." Maybe she said mongoloid, because I remember thinking she said he was foreign, Mongolian or Chinese.

Maybe he did not understand English, I thought, but, no, he had said, "Hey" to me.

Aunt Violet said Stevie lived with his sister Dulcie on the back side of the island. "Everyone knows Stevie," she said. Then it was like counting or conjugating.

"Everyone likes Stevie."

So I disliked him instantly. I went off to sleep thinking about the other boys I wanted to meet. Stevie didn't concern me.

Aunt Violet had said he was fifteen. Though he was older than me, he still acted like a baby. There was no reason to be envious of Stevie.

"Am-scray," I said when I saw him jump out of the dunes at me the next day. He looked amazed. I made shooing motions. "Get away from me."

But he followed at a distance as I took off after the other boys. I tracked them like a birder a rare species. Yet when I came upon them I was suddenly shy; too timid to look them in the eye. I went home picturing them. In my mind there were only blurs of light where their faces should have been.

The next morning, I got up early and went to the beach. I followed them, and that next evening I had fragments to put together like puzzle pieces in my memory.

I got braver as I got closer. I took in their shoulders, their chests, and their necks, but not their eyes. I looked down and was tickled to see the startling white gaps between the bottoms of the tans and their swim trunks.

I watched them again and almost felt pain at their clean lines and hard bodies. They were as unaware and sleek as seals as they moved from shore to water, and they were unaware of me.

Within a week I was adept at telling them apart. Three were blond, two had brown hair, and there was only one I did not like at all because he reminded me of myself. He had black hair and was a little flabby.

Ivan was not as graceful as the rest. He was square, with a barrel chest and big belly. When he fell off his skimboard or hiked up his bathing suit, he always looked around quickly to see if anyone noticed. Only I did, and when he saw me, Ivan glared as if I had pushed him, or it were my fault. I looked away when he came near.

When the others were nearby, though, I got giddy. Beach and day would disappear. It was not air; it was ether I breathed around them, another atmosphere. Since they wore dabs of suntan lotion on their shoulders and noses, I did too. I had to make do with substitutes. Crisco was all I could find.

"You trying to fry yourself?" Aunt Violet asked incredulously.

The boys were there when I closed my eyes at night; they were in my thoughts as I walked the beach. They got into my mind the way pollen gets into spring. I grew high like from sniffing gasoline. One blazing afternoon, Stevie stood up as if snapping to attention as I passed. I glared back suspiciously, for sometimes the kids at school made fun of the way I walked—with my arm bent up from the elbow and my hand leading as if I were a duchess expecting a courtier to kiss it. Stevie, however, just plodded on down the beach behind me.

I went right up to where those other boys, all of them, lay about, propped up on their elbows, looking out to sea.

The one named Jinx was closest: he had dark brown hair, an upturned nose and a light build. He stretched his leg out and wiggled his toes idly as he flung back his arms, yawning. He pulled something in me. I took my eyes off of him reluctantly.

I cleared my throat.

"Hi."

I looked to Billy. He was thick and had blondish-red hair and freckles. They called him "Little Billy"—to differentiate him from someone else. He had his back to me and languidly turned around to look my way.

I grew daring and took another step forward. Ivan sucked in his breath expectantly; he drew in his belly. But I passed by. Like a deputy from another planet, I went up to Glynn. I figured he was the leader.

He fascinated me, his dark muscular arms especially. Glynn was lying propped up on his elbows, looking out to sea.

He had a crew cut of white blond hair, which I could just barely see on his scalp. A faint scar on his right eyebrow kept it from forming perfectly, sort of cocking his face. The tip of his nose was red, and his eyes were cool and green. His gaze swept down his chest, taking in his own splendidness like a wealthy landowner surveying his property.

"Hello," I said to Glynn. "I'm just visiting here."

All the others watched as Glynn yawned and stretched.

He turned over on his stomach and snapped his blue elastic swimsuit. "Any of you guys hear anything?"

"Nope," Ivan said, smiling quickly. "Not me."

"Anybody see anything?"

"No."

Glynn turned and looked straight through me. He was so good, I couldn't refrain from smiling. I turned to Stevie and he smiled, too, nodding happily, as if he had witnessed something wonderful and was happy for me.

I sat down nearby, watching them. I had to show the boys that I could be a good sport, be the "hell of a good fellow," like Poppy's friends at Rotary.

Stevie grew tired of watching and went back to digging and building his dam across the gully. Soon Glynn and Jinx and the rest pushed off and I moved to where they had lain in the sand, glorying in the proximity. I closed my eyes—the sun reddened my lids as I saw how it would be.

One of the lesser boys—maybe Billy or Lee—would come across something like a piece of treasure, an ancient coin, a Civil War shell, or some pottery.

He'd pick it up and look at it curiously. A crowd would gather, but then a hush would spread and they would fall back as I appeared. They would get quieter still as I extended my hand, palm up. Billy would turn it over and fall back.

I would hold it to my forehead and think.

"It's an amphora, five thousand years old," I would say. "From Greece."

First they would gasp, then they would cheer. They would look around amazedly, just as I imagined those people in the room with Einstein must have done when he came up with his theories.

"Brain," they'd cry, or, "Genius!"

Jinx and Glynn would lift me up on their shoulders, and we would take off and do the wonderful things that kids did in Disney movies. It would be forever.

The siren shrieked and I woke up, looking all around me. Stevie was gone, I saw, and the boys had vanished down the beach. I started home for lunch.

I was happy on the street, reliving the dream. I stopped to squint: someone was on the porch with Aunt Violet.

I stamped my feet.

She was in her rocker, Stevie at her side, and they looked like beatniks with a big wooden bowl nearby. Both of them were snapping beans.

Not again, I thought. Not like Otis! I turned around quickly.

One day back home, Otis had caught up with me on the road. I had blown my bike tire filling it at the gas station, and the mechanics there had laughed at me. I was wheeling it along and Otis followed. He did not say a thing. If I ran ahead, he would catch up; if I slowed down, he would not pass.

When we reached his gate, he stopped; I looked back. He looked so pitiful, it stung me.

"Oh, all right," I said, putting my bike down. I looked around to see if anyone was watching.

We went into his house, through a closet of his mother's dresses, to the attic, where he turned on his trains and let them circle around in figure eights. He smiled wetly and licked his lips when the whistles shrieked.

Whenever he saw me after that he would say hello. And when his father drove down Main Street in his pickup, Otis stood in the back, waving like a beauty queen. He'd holler out my name for everybody to hear.

"I saw your friend today," Francine would say with eyes agleam.

So I decided *not again*, as I stood there on the melting tar street. I would not be duped again with Stevie. I turned back toward the beach.

But up on the porch, Aunt Violet caught sight of me.

"Yoo-hoo," she screeched. "You!"

I stopped, puzzled. There was something in her voice I had not heard before—as if she were a girl flirting with me.

I edged up the walkway.

"There you are," she cried as happily as a little girl in make-believe. "Look who's here!"

She flung her arms out and stepped back like a housewife advertising a lemon-scented product on TV. "It's Stevie!"

Aunt Violet looked back and forth between us as if she expected a chemical reaction to take place right before her eyes, or maybe we were touched with Crazy Glue and would bond instantly.

I grimaced because she didn't know that she had broken a taboo, that there was an understanding between me and Stevie—like the one between blacks and whites in the city. We knew our rankings, knew how we should be. Stevie on the beach had been content to get what reception I had given him. But now he smiled and raised his eyebrows in a gesture like begging.

"Hey," I said.

"Hi."

Stevie smiled sweetly at me. And Aunt Violet was so happy.

We stood there, no one doing anything, Stevie's smile getting bigger and bigger. It was her fondness of him that set me off.

"Pardon me, won't you?" I said. "I have to pee."

Stevie giggled.

I went to the kitchen for a drink.

A second later, Aunt Violet stormed in. She put the bowl of beans down on the counter. I looked at her but didn't say a word. She took her purse.

Leaving the room, she shot me a hot glance. I went to the window to look.

She fished out a nickel and put it in Stevie's hand. Curling his fingers around it, she said, "You take this down to the store and give it to the girl for ice cream. You hear?"

Never had she given me money. "No snacks between meals," was what she told me.

I watched Stevie accept the gift, looking up at her like a baby bird at its mother.

"Don't you worry," Aunt Violet said, getting up from where she had crouched. "That nasty boy didn't mean a thing."

He nodded again, believing her eagerly.

She pushed him toward the stairs and waved when he reached the street. She turned around and came in. Her smile disappeared altogether when she saw me.

She started to speak, but picked up the bowl again. I started into the next room when Aunt Violet reached out and spun me around. She held my chin.

"Why did you do that?" she asked abruptly.

"Do what?"

"Don't you—"

"I had to go to the bathroom—"

"You evil thing," she shrieked, and then slapped me. "Evil!" The suddenness even seemed to surprise her. She looked at her hand in horror as if it had acted independently.

My eyes started to fill, and that made Aunt Violet angrier.

"Don't you do that! You will be nice to Stevie," she said. "You hear?"

She made a vise of her bony hands and shook me. "Understand?"

"No," I shouted.

She shoved me and turned her hands on herself, closing them on her face as if in prayer or hiding. I felt I had been flung out of her hand like trash. Every sorrow I had ever felt rushed in to crush me.

I ran to the bathroom. Uncle Reynaldo stood in the hall behind the door and reached out.

"Boy," he said gently.

But I shoved him. "Get away," I screamed.

Locked in the bathroom, I cried and cried. Much

later, I washed my face. I sat on the floor listening to Aunt Violet's sobs.

"Oh, Rennie," she said. "He's a monster. A beast."

"There, there," I heard him say. I imagined his tears.

Aunt Violet's anger I could take. I wanted her to hit me again so I could report her to Momma. I watched her icily that evening. But the reproach I saw in Uncle Reynaldo's face was too much. It ate at me.

I went to bed that night still upset, planning how I could get even with Stevie. I dreamed of flamboyant schemes, as elaborate and complex as perpetual-motion machines, complete with cannon and pits and Ferris wheels, to torture him exquisitely.

I'd have revenge, I vowed, and I'd get the boys to like me. Together, we'd all be mean to Stevie.

I FOLLOWED THEM ON THE beach the next morning, smiling my best smile, laughing at their jokes. I dropped money but let them keep it. I followed them shamelessly, until they tired of teasing me. Except Ivan. He was scared, looking at me as if I was a hole he could fall in; as if he could become me.

I encroached on them in the day and planned in the evenings. I lay on my bed and I heard them as they called out for each other—for Billy and Glynn and Jinx and Lee. My head swam and the air became luminous with possibility.

The names they called had shapes to them—like stars, lightning bolts, or baseball bats. I loved the sounds, for not a one of them had a creepy name like mine. Leaning out the window, I could feel them pulling me to them, to the future, under the gold-green trees.

I followed.

"What's wrong with you?" Aunt Violet asked me one night as I bumped into her table, jiggling the light she read by. I was listening to the boys as if they were calling me by name.

"Quit walking around here like a zombie," she said. "And don't slam the screen."

Out on the porch I heard her muttering. But I saw the boys going down a path to the beach. I ran after them. *This is it*, I told myself. *Tonight*.

Night was nigh. It was not falling—or if it was, it was like dots, the way I imagined radioactivity: little dots of darkness getting closer and closer, making the light disappear. Night seemed to flow upward, rising like a mist from the sea.

I scampered to catch up with them. All over the beach, knots of people in groups of twos or threes walked with shuttered lanterns in search of turtles climbing out of the sea.

A few came every night. Out of the surf, pulled by the lights or by instinct. They came up to lay their eggs high in the sand dunes; then they crawled back to the sea.

"Why do people watch?" I asked Uncle Reynaldo one evening.

"To count," he answered.

"Why?"

"Because they're endangered."

I didn't understand.

"They might become extinct," he explained. "Never, ever touch one. Treat it gently."

So when I saw one of them, I gave it a wide berth—though not that night.

I knew as soon as I got close that the boys had found one. They were in a circle around it.

I inched forward and passed into their midst as if into

a circle of light and heat. Excitement rose in a glow around me, tightening my throat so that I could barely breathe.

I listened. They all stood around the great black thing.

"It's stopped moving."

Glynn poked it.

"What's it doing?"

"It's taking a dump," Billy said disgustedly and turned away.

"No! It . . . it's laying eggs!" Jinx shrieked. I loved looking at him—he seemed so happy. I was too, just watching. I wanted Jinx to like me.

Billy snapped the flashlight on, and they all kneeled around it like kids in a manger scene.

"There! Look," they said, pointing: a religious hush spread and the light picked out the oozing, gelatinous things.

"Wow!"

Glynn's face wavered in the light: smooth, perfect, and uncaring.

For a moment we were silent, looking at the mysterious, shiny things.

But then they picked up my scent; I could feel the boys stiffening.

"What are *you* doing here?" Jinx asked.

I could not speak. . . .

Everyone looked my way. I just shrugged. The boys regrouped. Ivan turned the light on me.

Rising to my feet, I put my hand out but Glynn pushed.

Ivan had crouched down on all fours behind me. I rolled toward the turtle. The earth swung on its axis with a nightmarish quality.

I was falling toward the back of the beast as it pushed away. I reached, but fell into the indentation in the sand. Rubbery things oozed in my shoe.

I jumped up, brushing myself off and screaming.

They shouted.

"He's broken them!" "He's killed them!" But it was even worse when they turned the light on my face.

"Ugh," they screamed.

"It was an accident," I pleaded. "You all made me do it! You pushed me!"

In the wobbling light, they grew angry.

I looked up to Jinx and stretched out my arm for him to pull me away.

"Please," I said.

The light rippled over his narrow face like a candle, and I could see him considering. His smile grew and then he made a sign to someone behind me.

I turned around and he pushed. This time I fell forward into the sand.

I tried to get up, but Jinx pounced and held me down. I laid my face on my hands and sobbed.

Like giants, I felt them looking down on me. "Damn crybaby," they said disgustedly. "Won't even fight."

"He's no fun."

"Let's get out of here."

I was going to get up, but Ivan came back and spit on me.

"There," he said. "Crybaby."

By the time I went down to the water, the turtle had already gone back to the sea.

I was sick the next day—with regret, with worry—that I had destroyed a whole species single-handedly. I avoided the boys though we all knew we had a rendez-vous. We all knew it was just a matter of time until they got me.

A few days later when I went back, there was a carcass of a sea turtle stranded up high on the beach. I stayed clear, but the other boys went to examine it. When they turned it over, a huge column of flies rose up.

I ran when they saw me.

I waited with dread. As I walked the green lanes, I accepted it unquestioningly.

I knew the moment was coming that morning on the beach as they appeared low on the horizon. The tide, going out, had even taken away the breeze. The airlessness of the moment, its brightness, gave it a shimmering, out-of-time quality.

Stevie felt it, too. He stood up and watched as Glynn and the rest of them started my way. For once, Ivan was leading.

I stood up and awaited them.

They stopped, unsure and curious that I did not run. I faced them as if facing a firing squad.

Ivan backed up.

"One, two . . ." he counted, then they all stepped back and swung their arms like windmills as he cried, "Doo! Doo!"

The dirt slammed my face; my glasses flew from my ringing ears; clods thundered around me. There was mud mixed in with the dead turtle in my mouth, slime down my back, and grit against my teeth. It was me, all right, but somehow it was not happening.

Was it like *extinct*? I wondered if that was why the Carolina Paroquet stood so still—amazed that it could have been left out, that the cosmos could continue on its way, disregarding it totally.

I turned to look at the boys, and they looked back. Their smiles shrank. Their teasing sputtered and failed.

They backed away.

I stood there, stunned at the disparity of what I had dreamed and what was happening. The earth stopped and something from the corner of my eye swept toward us. It was Stevie; he had watched the whole thing.

"That was bad!" he shouted, and he flung himself at Glynn. He made fists and beat on him. "That was mean!"

Glynn was shocked. With a cry, he reached out and caught both of Stevie's hands in one of his. But Stevie lunged and Glynn swung his whole body in the other direction. Both lurched off balance. It looked like they were dancing.

"Whoa, Stevie!"

Glynn broke free, but Stevie circled back. There were tears streaming down his face. He rushed at the boys and they backed off, cheering.

Stevie was going to rush at Ivan, but just then lost his balance. He fell to the ground so suddenly, we could hear his teeth click. He looked up dumbfounded.

"You OK, Stevie?" They rushed up, worried.

Jinx pulled him to his feet. Stevie lunged at them again and they jumped back. He veered toward me, his face wet and lips quivering.

"Good boy, Stevie," Ivan laughed. "You take care of your friend."

He was trying to: he was coming up to me. But I was disgusted and pushed him away.

"Drop dead," I shouted. He and the rest of them all stopped, amazed, and looked at me.

Stevie had a dazed look on his face, and the boys were rallying around him as I left.

"You OK?" they asked. Jinx had his arm around him and Ivan patted him on the back.

"That-a-boy," they said.

He said something and they laughed at it good-naturedly.

"Come on," they said, moving off together toward the gully. "Let's help Stevie with his dam."

Stevie looked up dazed as they pulled him along. Best of friends, they splashed down in the water.

"Meany," they said, looking up at me.

I watched in disbelief. He had stolen my place. I should have been there with them, not Stevie.

The rest of the day, I lay on my bed, staring at the ceiling. As day grayed into evening, I got an idea.

I went back to the beach.

The water was the color of pewter, and against it the dark of Stevie's dam in the gully stood out starkly. Storm clouds were coming.

For weeks Stevie had been trying to close off one end of the gully and now it was done. The sticks they had put on top of it looked like soldiers.

"Isn't it nice?" I said tartly. The thought of Stevie's happy face prodded me. I started picking at the dam with my toes, just flicking little clods of earth into the water, watching them dissolve. The sticks that fell floated like bodies. I burrowed a little deeper, but I started to hurry.

I got madder and madder, and as I kicked, I got faster. I couldn't control myself. I bent down, clawing and growling. A vision of the boys goaded me.

Just before the dam dissolved, the urgent water hovered like an animal about to spring.

"Take that!" I cried ecstatically. "Take that!" Lightning flashed and I was exultant. The dam broke and water gushed out.

It started raining.

IT STORMED THAT NIGHT. Rain drummed the windows and dribbled through the ceiling. I stayed up listening to it dripping into pots and reading tabloids that Aunt Violet had put on the floor and I rescued; tabloids that had a series on the ghosts of Dixie. They showed men with no heads walking under magnolia trees, and white wraiths waiting for soldiers murdered by Yankees. The yellow bedside lamp cast a warmth and I felt safe and cozy knowing that outside, water was rising.

In the morning, I crept out to see. Dread hit me. Stevie was already there.

I had heard he had a sister. I thought she would be just like him, only bigger. But she was different; Dulcie's hair was blond. She had a colorless complexion and eyes the shade of washed jeans. She was as amorphous as a dumpling. Dulcie had the perpetual look of having just shrugged; her arms dangled loosely. But soon she was kneeling and had her arms around Stevie. He hooked his chin over her shoulder so I saw his back and Dulcie looking at me incuriously—not in anger or even in sadness, but in acceptance, as if inviting me to surrender.

Maybe it was the clothes she wore—white knee socks, a white blouse and a plaid skirt with a big wooden pin— she looked like a huge girl. She tried to get up, but Stevie clung to her so tightly she tipped. He had his arms around her neck now as if he were drowning.

I choked up, for I could see how he had brought Dulcie down to show off his dam. I hated myself for feeling weak but I did not like to think that anyone could be that unhappy. With that familiar sense of worthlessness, I could feel myself weakening even further.

I knew if any of the kids in school had done this, they would have fled. Francine would have. But not me. What I was doing made no sense, but I could not help myself. Defeat for me was like gravity.

Dulcie blinked. I moved closer.

She stood up to release him and Stevie turned around. His eyes were bruised with grief, but he would not lift them to me.

"I know who did it," I said. "It wasn't the storm."

"Who?" He looked up then.

"Glynn."

His eyes widened, thrilled, and I nodded. "And Jinx helped. I saw them. I tried to make them stop. I did. . . ."

I did not know where the words were coming from, but I believed them suddenly. My voice broke.

"But they—they hit me."

Stevie nodded. He smiled beatifically.

"Come on," I said. "We'll build it back."

Stevie looked at Dulcie. She nodded and then he took

my hand. I took him down to the gully. All day as we built
it back, he kept looking my way, happily, shyly, as if I were
important.

Everything was different suddenly.

Aunt Violet was odd that night when she saw us come
home, and was that next morning, too, when she woke
me. Usually she poked and prodded, getting pleasure out
of wresting me from sleep. But that morning she just stood
there in the doorway gazing at my bed adoringly.

"He's here," she said when I opened my eyes. She
ran away as nervous and fluttery as a bird.

She flew to the kitchen; I went out to the middle room
and saw something at the back door. Without my glasses
it looked fuzzy against the green, like a big fish floating in
an aquarium. I squinted. Stevie had his hands over his eyes
as he peered in.

My first instinct was to dart into the bathroom and
lock the door. I wouldn't answer, I told myself, when Aunt
Violet rapped. I pictured her getting the fire department
to come, or Stevie himself. Acting as a battering ram, he'd
run through the house as Aunt Violet shouted, "Heave!"

"Ho!"

He'd fly in as the door buckled and popped off its
hinges, and Stevie would land—plop—on top of me.

I gave up and went to the kitchen. Like a flower lifting
its face to the sun, Stevie looked up from his plate at me.

Aunt Violet and Uncle Reynaldo looked at me dif-
ferently, as if I had changed and they were now intrigued
with me. It was as if the air had turned cool: there was a
different feeling in the room suddenly.

"Isn't this nice?" Aunt Violet asked.

Uncle Reynaldo smiled and I smiled back to make
peace. He ruffled Stevie's hair and waved at us as we went
down the steps.

"You two have fun," he said.

I turned back to see Aunt Violet leaning against the column with a dreamy look on her face like someone watching a sunset or a romantic movie.

I stayed with Stevie that day because of this.

And I stayed with him the following days because it was easy. I did not have to show off. He was fat, had droopy girl-like titties, and wore a white T-shirt when he went in swimming. I could be myself around Stevie.

Which meant I could be mean. But I was careful not to let Aunt Violet see. I took the inner tube he brought for himself after he rolled it down the street to the beach.

"It's mine," I said, getting into it. He just shook his head.

"Yes it is."

He looked away, smiling as if I were doing something tricky.

When I got out of the water and started digging a hole, the inner tube drifted off. He went in after it while I ignored him.

"Come on," he said, handing it over.

"I don't want it."

"Please."

So I took it to make him happy.

That afternoon, I told Stevie stories. I rattled off my thoughts, telling him about my folks, Francine, our cat, Binky. I told him things Francine had done, passing them off as if they had happened to me, and I could see him picturing them. I began to believe in them, too, because of Stevie. He listened to me, sitting rapt, eyes wide and his mouth open, as if I were a wise man passing on the oral history of a whole civilization.

It was funny: summer, so ghostly, so wordless before in those empty streets, now began to take on dimension. After lunch I went looking for him. I liked being with

Stevie. I looked forward to the next morning. Aunt Violet and Uncle Reynaldo were proud of me.

Every day we paraded like sentries along the shore as the scenery repeated as it does in cartoons. The same houses and trees on one side, the sea on the other.

I told Stevie things about it, too—things that I had read coming back to me. I told him about Atlantis, that there was another world mirroring ours under the water, and how it would rise one day. I stood up as I said it.

So did he.

The water would rush off it, I told him, and then everything else would drown. I could see his face delighted with fear.

After that, when he saw a submarine coming from the navy base, he got excited and pointed.

"Atlantis!" he screamed. "I want to go there!"

Every item he found on the beach carried significance then: light bulbs, empty bottles of bleach. They had bobbed up from the world under the sea.

"It's from Atlantis," he'd say, holding a bottle in front of my face like a trophy. When I would mutter, "No, I don't think so," his face would fall and he'd drop the thing and walk away sullenly.

So I relented sometimes and said, "Maybe it is."

Then Stevie danced with the bottle in his hand and begged me to tell him how Atlantis would be. It was upside down, I said; everyone was rich and people walked on ceilings.

I talked and he listened, nodding his head as he did when he was eating to show that he was still listening; and like the blind, he had to touch me when I was near. But I had to stop, because Atlantis began to scare me.

Stevie did not know it was make-believe; he kept wanting to go there in his inner tube. He went out too deep, to where Jinx and Glynn and the rest of them swam.

I was confused being around them when I was with Stevie. So I called him in.

"Come on, Stevie," I cried from the shore.

I was cross with him and did not answer his questions. He took off then and left me, as he did when I told him things that were upsetting.

Once I told him about Siamese twins. I had read of them in the tabloids, and what I didn't know I fabricated.

I told Stevie they could never be separated. If one died first, the other one had to drag the dead one around with him. When the dead one's hand started to rot, so did the living one's. I grabbed his hand and held it to mine.

"Like this, Stevie," I said, stroking the back of his hand.

"No," he screamed.

He pulled away and stopped and looked around as if he heard someone call. That spooked me. "What is it?" I asked, but he took off running.

"Stevie!" I cried. "Come back!"

I went after him, but by the time I reached the street, he was gone. I felt abandoned, as if summer and time were both my fault, as if I had spilled them and they were spreading uncontrollably.

I wandered back home. My opening the door woke Aunt Violet and she asked, "Where's Stevie?"

"Nowhere."

I went back to my room and tried to open the drawer. But it was stuck shut like a tomb. The boys could not help me. I went back outside.

I clung to the porch railing, looking. The street stretched out for miles in both directions. A car went by in a bright gleam.

I decided that afternoon I should be nice to Stevie.

———

A few days later when he saw some dead fish in the gully, Stevie took off again. He skittered along frantically and I followed him until he rounded the corner of a street and paused when he saw a sway-backed house that I found out was his. Once he got closer, he started running toward it as urgently as if he had to pee.

I ran along, too, because the back side of the island scared me.

Our side, the sea side, had big white summer houses with high roofs swooping low over porches. But on the marsh side of the island where Stevie lived, the houses were close together and unpainted and unrelieved by any breeze. Back there the shacks had that beaten hound dog look; they crouched under chinaberry trees with roofs that were red and rust-streaked. The front porches held old iceboxes and wringer washing machines; there were flowers growing in tin cans, while the yards were grassless and swept clean. The people on the back side of Sullivan's Island lived there all year and grew not flowers in their gardens but okra, tomatoes, water-melons, and green beans. At the corner of the street where we turned was a house with a splayed picket fence and a little blond girl playing in dirt packed so hard it was shiny. She wore a T-shirt but no pants, and her face was dirty.

"Lookit," she cried when we went by. She turned up her face and smiled at us so widely, it scrunched up her features; she seemed deformed with happiness. She whirled around and fell down dizzily.

Once Stevie made it into his house, he was better. He went off into the kitchen and called for Dulcie. If she was not there (and she rarely was during the week, because she took the bus downtown to her job at Woolworth's), he'd go stand in her room. He lifted the top to her white powder dish, touched her glass poodles, smelled her perfume, and opened her lipstick. The room was dim and I rarely went in. When he came out, he was calmed and asked me to get him something to eat.

It became a routine after swimming. One day he was sitting and watching TV in the room that had once been a porch; creepers and vines grew down the screens. A radio turned on; I didn't think anything about it as I made our bologna sandwiches. But then the back door opened.

I expected Dulcie, but it was a man.

"Your sister back?" he asked Stevie.

Stevie shook his head.

The man was dark and looked mean. He went to the refrigerator and took out a beer.

"What you looking at?" he asked.

"Nothing." I swallowed and looked down.

The man grunted and took a slice of bread and rolled it over a piece of bologna from Stevie's plate. He stuffed them in his mouth and said something I couldn't understand.

"Who's he?" I asked when he left.

"Leroy," Stevie said.

"Who's Leroy?"

"Dulcie's boyfriend," he answered.

"Leroy," I thought, going to the window. He made my throat dry and my heart beat. I suppose it was his rudeness, his dangerousness, and his dark eyes that attracted me. He wore a V-neck T-shirt, blue jeans, and pointy boots; his hair hung over his forehead in a wave like Elvis Presley's.

I knew Momma would have latched the screen if Leroy had come up on our back porch and asked her something.

That evening when I went over, I saw Leroy and Dulcie on the porch. Leroy was sitting on a chair tilted back against the wall, smoking a cigarette. Dulcie was close by, her hands clasped together, forgetful of the dishtowel she was holding. I crept up to watch something illicit, impressing it on my mind, as if it would become my testimony.

Dulcie went back into the kitchen and came out a little later and stood behind him, her hair flowing down over her face the way willow trees hung over the houses. She laughed and pulled away when she saw me. But Leroy pulled her back to his lap and kissed the back of her neck till she flopped around like a rag doll.

Leroy changed everything. Within a few weeks of his coming, cars up on blocks with no wheels appeared. Leroy supposedly fixed things, but it seemed that once in the yard, the cars never left. As if they had some sort of emblematic quality for him, Leroy stood looking at the cars as if they were a crop he had grown. Occasionally he sat behind the wheel of one, staring out through the glassless windshield.

When Leroy was around, I tried to get his attention. I made noises, I wiggled my ears.

Leroy would look at me like I was crazy.

"C'mon, Dull," he'd say after supper and pinch the back of her neck and whisper in her ear.

They'd go into her room and lock the door, and I'd strain for sounds as I sat with Stevie in front of the TV. Later, I'd hear the door open. Leroy would leave and I would tiptoe over and peer into Dulcie's room while she showered, taking in the dimness, the unmade bed, and closed blinds. I sensed something momentous had just happened, but I did not know what and it troubled me.

Stevie would call out and I'd go back. After hours of game shows, we'd turn the television off and go outside, blinking in the twilight, suddenly real.

We'd go past the Red and White, the liquor store, and the pharmacy. On the corner of Middle Street was a gas station with a green dinosaur on its sign under which people gathered. I was shy if we saw Leroy in the crowd, but Stevie thought nothing of pestering him for money. Then we'd march up to the old Coke machine and turn the crank handle, once for him and once for me. The drinks tickled our throats.

The lights in the filling station stayed on until ten. A bell rang when cars drove in, and colored plastic pennants snapped in the breeze, giving it a carnival atmosphere. Leroy lounged about with his friends, watching old, fat Mr. Redmond in his office, the window's fluorescent glare looming bright in the evening. Mr. Redmond sat in his chair spreading his legs out with his hands to accommodate his vast belly. Tipping back, he took a sip from his flask and then wiped his mouth. He licked his fingers and moved his lips as he bent over his cigar box and counted his money. Like a sycophant, a little fan danced attendance on him, turning this way and that. There were always dark stains on his shirt and Mr. Redmond was always sweating.

When he waved them in, Leroy and his friends filed in one by one like children, removing their painter's hats and accepting the flask. They nudged each other and told jokes that made him gasp—that was Mr. Redmond's way of laughing. Stevie and I would sneak in, wondering which trick or joke or ploy would coax a laugh from Mr. Redmond and prompt him to pass more whiskey.

Sometimes they even gave us a sip; they always gave it first to Stevie, who took it happily. He passed it my way and I accepted it like it was communion or something. Leroy's friends were nicer to Stevie than they were to me. They treated him the way they would an old dog, saying things like, "You doing OK, boy?" while they patted his head.

"They doing right by you, Stevie?"

When he answered, though, they were not really listening.

Occasionally one of them would pick up one of the

*Playboy*s on Mr. Redmond's desk and flash it open at Stevie and ask, "Getting any?"

Stevie blushed crimson, shaking his head, and everyone laughed. Mr. Redmond would turn redder still and made a gurgling sound like he was dying.

I tried to show them that it pained me; they noted my reaction and thought it was funny. Leroy looked at me as if he had just seen something flash across my face. I was breathless and tried to do it again to get him to look at me.

I looked at them almost lovingly, but the only time that whole summer that Leroy ever looked at me with anything close to affection was when I surprised him once in Dulcie's room.

He jumped when I came in to fetch something. I was about to say, "Excuse me," but he held a finger to his lips. "Shh," he cautioned, and pulled me into the conspiracy. He picked up Dulcie's purse and extracted her wallet— he pulled out a ten-dollar bill. Then he winked and said, "Don't tell her." He stuck his hand back in and gave a dollar to me.

When Mr. Redmond did not invite the men in, they gathered behind the cinder-block building and passed a bottle along surreptitiously, keeping it low, hidden from the police.

Sometimes a car horn beeped. At the wheel would be one of the men from the front of the island; Leroy and his friends came to attention begrudgingly as the one summoned wiped his hands on the back of his pants and swaggered over. The man in the driver's seat would smile and joke, but it was as if he was begging.

"My wife," he would begin as a way of apology. He'd look up at Leroy or one of his friends almost pleadingly, explaining what chore was needed—roofing or yard work or plumbing. "Could you come . . . I mean, if you're free?"

They talked on some more after they struck the deal, about a ball game or the weather or fishing, the engine idling all the while. Then the man would drive off looking relieved, and the summoned man would come to the wall. He'd say something and they would all laugh obscenely.

If anyone had to pee, he rarely went inside to that foul-smelling bathroom; more than likely he just unzipped his pants and stood along the fence swamped in honey-suckle and ivy, continuing to speak while the smell of urine and sweetness rose up dizzingly. Some of the men stroked themselves down there when they were finished, as if it were their best friend they were attending. Others, how-ever, just pulled up their zippers like starting a chain saw. A morbid fascination held me—until suddenly I had to get away.

"Stevie," I'd say. "Come here." But Stevie would be out of touch, buzzing nonsense under his breath. "You sending messages to Mars?"

Often I actually had to pull him from the spot to get him going.

We plunged down lanes, suddenly mysterious in the eve-ning, past dark houses with only faint ghosts of flickering lights from TVs as people sat on screen porches, mumbling vague things, like just before sleep.

If Glynn and Jinx biked along, I got confused and scared. I darted into a bush like a rabbit being chased by a dog or a soldier being strafed from the air by the enemy. I did not want to be around them anymore. Stevie followed me. Such antics made him happy.

We went to his house to resume the endless game of Monopoly. We returned to it like it was an obligation or a duty. Then, if it was all right with Dulcie, Stevie came home and spent the night with me.

Uncle Reynaldo spoke to us on the porch while Aunt Violet listened from the kitchen. We went for late walks, and after Aunt Violet and Uncle Reynaldo went to sleep, we lay awake. Stevie asked about all manner of things—about Jesus, Atlantis (Was it Atlantis?), and TV until we ran down like clocks and drifted off to sleep.

When it was too hot, we sneaked out of the house, crouching low under the windows like thieves. There was an undertow that pulled swimmers to the jetties—those jagged rocks that ringed the harbor mouth like sharks' teeth; so were we pulled out of our beds at night to the beach. I looked back in the moonlight, half expecting to see myself still lying in bed, for the night made things seem as eerie as trips outside my body.

We were not alone. People came out from town every night. Stevie and I went in swimming, waving around in the phosphorescence to make streaks. He wanted to stay out all night, to swim to Atlantis, but I wouldn't let him. I had to pull him back to the shore, and since we could not shower without waking Reynaldo and Violet, we lay together salty until morning. But nights on the beach when storms came up were different stories.

I liked them, for they changed everything: they cleared the air and charged it with electricity.

Stevie did not like storms, however. He was afraid of lightning. He'd run back to the house from the beach and wait on the porch for me. When I came up, he ran in quickly and dove under the covers. Stevie sat in bed with his back to the wall, his eyes wide with fear. If I called from the window, he would not answer.

"Come on," I cried.

I felt as if the storm were a whirlwind that had come up to take me someplace exciting, and if I didn't watch out, it would spin off without me.

"Stevie, please."

I told him he was silly: I had Uncle Reynaldo tell him it was not so, but he believed that if he made noise in a thunderstorm, he would get hit by lightning. I even disproved it, calling out his name when the bright flare came. He panicked and burrowed under the bedding.

"Oh, come on out."

I was angry as I went back into the house. I thought he was trying to take away the one thing that made me happy, but turning back and seeing him under the sheets made me give in. Lightning hit, the room spun with shadows, and I held on to the sill as if on a rearing ship plunging through the billows and crests of a shadow sea. I saw his eyes, thin crescents of fear.

"Oh, Stevie!"

I went back to bed and held him. When the thunder shook, I petted his back and said, "Don't worry."

Something warm rose as he bumped against me; I could feel the pull between us, its magnetism like static electricity. I felt proud that I could be so grown-up and comfort Stevie.

For hours, as the storm came up and light and darkness crashed around us, we held on to each other like Siamese twins. Occasionally he peeped out to see which side, light or darkness, was winning.

The storms always passed. The house shook less; the rain got gentler; the frogs started to croak and then Stevie's breathing grew deep.

"See, Stevie?" I said when it was over. "Let's go out!"

I turned to look at him and he fell away, mouth open, arms loose, asleep. I watched him in the cool, chastened air until sleep got me, too.

By morning we had forgotten it all as we ran to see what was washed up on the beach. But when another storm came up to wake us in the middle of the night, we suddenly were back in the same warm feeling, like Indian summer, or remembering. We held hands. I looked at him and he looked back. As we nestled each other, everything else fell away.

Those were the moments we were real.

We were together all we could be. In the evenings we went walking and Uncle Reynaldo pointed out things: snakes garlanded over branches like bright necklaces or birds camouflaged in trees. Once or twice he pointed out shiny things that proved to be dimes; more often than not, however, they were foil nothings.

One night as we walked down the island's last forested street, Uncle Reynaldo pointed his stick at a tall cast-iron gate. A tunnel seemed to lead from it, dark and choked with green.

Down there, he said, he had found the Carolina Paroquet. He sounded sad, and Stevie came up and stood beside him. But Uncle Reynaldo did not seem to see him or me; instead he was looking on into history. There was a graveyard down there, he said, by the ruins of an old pest house where people had been kept in quarantine.

Earlier there had been a *baracoon* for penning slaves brought from Africa. I thought we were going down there to see it all: I had pictures in my mind of the ghosts of Dixie. They had looked like the hostesses on the social pages, all white and flowing.

But Uncle Reynaldo turned us around. I turned back and saw the open gate and the light through the trees.

"Come on." Uncle Reynaldo motioned. "Violet's waiting."

I wanted to go back, but we never went down that street again. Instead, Uncle Reynaldo took us crabbing and into old forts with dripping tunnels in them. He sent us down the blocks of the island, called stations from the island's military history, to where we could find things. We'd ask him about them when we came back in the evening.

One night when we came, he gave us each a firefly. They rose up, but they did not get away; he had tied them with string.

They haloed us with a light like our special feeling. We were tied, too; there was nowhere else I wanted to be than with Stevie.

By the end of summer I realized how much I had changed. I was not concerned when Glynn and his friends came by. Ivan could stick out his tongue, but I ignored it. Jinx no longer held an attraction for me.

Instead I looked forward to Stevie coming over. Uncle Reynaldo came out then and sat on the porch and we listened. It was like one of those walks we took with him—he'd pause, backtrack, and sometimes lose the trail entirely.

He'd hold his finger to his lips to silence us before beginning. We were as excited as if everything we had done that summer had brought us to this moment, as if we were getting ready for what we would hear. Aunt Violet would watch from the window above the sink.

He'd speak in his old, slow voice, not of once-upon-a-time but of *used-to-be*. He'd look at us, and as he spoke, it seemed he was changing, getting stronger and younger by remembering.

We listened as Aunt Violet finished the dishes. Then, like a fawn drawn out of the woods, she, too, would come out slowly.

It was lulling, listening. It was the past he spoke of mostly, and it was as eerie and wonderful as the music that Francine and I listened to on the radio as it spun out of nothingness from across the dark prairie. He told us marvelous things—his voice softened and there was something in his eyes then like unseen sunsets reflected in windows of west-facing buildings.

He spoke of a time when people were kinder, politer: they believed in things. Paroquets still lived in the trees. But people made mistakes, he said, that still needed fixing.

"We have to be nice to each other—to coloreds and to whites," he said one night, and explained. Charleston had been awful; the people had done evil, they had waged a war for slavery. Some of their children's children still believed in the old ideas, he told us: the ideas, like viruses, were still around, infecting. That was why he and Aunt Violet had left. Now that they were back, they were waiting, with Lula and her friends, for healing, for a better day to come. As if recruiting, he looked at us wistfully.

Aunt Violet would start up then. Pushing at her rocking chair with her palms on its arms and her feet on the floor, she'd tip way back and close her eyes.

"A new day," she'd say, rocking. "A new day is coming."

The way she described it, we could see it rising like Atlantis from the sea. Coloreds would sit down with whites; together we'd break chains and change history. Uncle Reynaldo would nod his head and stroke his lap as if there were a cat on it, and we would see a city rising up and triumphing over its past. We could keep the feeling among us if we did not speak.

One night Aunt Violet, Uncle Reynaldo, Stevie, and I all went down to the beach. Stevie and I saw something huge and glistening rise in the surf. We ran out to it, but it disappeared. We came back and Uncle Reynaldo pointed down at our feet: we were in the midst of tracks that looked like those of a jeep. It was where a turtle had come up from the water and laid her eggs near the dunes before returning.

I felt strange then, as if there was something I had to remember, as if something I had been searching for all summer had taken shape and was now within reach. Something in the air chilled me.

I thought of Francine. If only we could be nice to each other, I thought. *If only.* And I thought of Otis Farrabee and felt as sad and thrilled as I did back home listening to the whippoorwills calling. I'll be good, I promised silently.

I realized I had slipped away from the world I was from, to the one by the sea, a world of books and goodness and puffed sleeves, of kind people and the paroquet. I wanted to be friends with Otis and Stevie and Lula no matter what people thought. It was so simple, so easy.

I looked to Aunt Violet and Uncle Reynaldo and Stevie. They were looking up in the sky, awash with a billion dots of light. I stared, and it was as if all the stars came spiraling down, whirring in a blur like the Milky Way, around me. It was as if the sky had opened for me.

I gasped, realizing that until that summer I had been afraid of understanding. Other kids' parents would always say, "Oh, it's OK if there's not enough cake to go around. You can skip *him*," they'd say, meaning me. "He's so understanding." I thought understanding was a consolation prize, a gag gift for not winning. But that night under the stars, I did not feel weak. I understood that it was more important to be good than be happy. Aunt Violet and Uncle Reynaldo had been trying to teach me this all summer long, I saw suddenly.

So I turned to them, my eyes brimming. I wanted to tell them that I understood, but they were still watching the sky. Their heads were up and their eyes were filled with light. They knew already.

IT TURNED COOL SOON
after. Uncle Reynaldo said it was August's cool week,
the time that came as a brief respite each year. We walked
on into it as if into wisdom or a clearing, for summer was
no longer thick and hot and clouded with misunder-
standing.

Moving through the water the night before I left,
Stevie and I left pale phosphorescent streaks. It was almost
too late for turtles, but we saw one up high by the dunes.

It was dark—no one else was near.

Stevie squatted on his haunches in front of the turtle
and blew on its flesh, as ancient and withered as an
elephant's.

Its yellow eye opened.

"What's wrong?" he wanted to know.

"Maybe it's stuck," I said. Stevie bent down to look.

The turtle opened and shut its eyes again and moved its flippers as Stevie tentatively touched it.

"It *is* stuck," he said. He started pushing. I approached gingerly, but pitched in.

It was slow going. We stopped and started, looking back now and again to measure the distance we had shoved the dead weight down the beach—it seemed to stretch on endlessly. Finally, the sand got wetter and the turtle's flippers moved as if trying to catch hold of something. We were exhausted when we reached the water and pushed it in.

We stood there expectantly. Stevie shouted, "Get going, turtle, please."

He climbed on top of it in desperation and kicked it with his heel.

I tried to take him off.

But then there was a release like a groan, and a shudder. I cried and jumped back as the beast's flipper grazed my leg. I spun around to see Stevie flying into the water, spray unfurling behind him, his eyes alight.

I panicked and rushed to save him.

"Stevie!" I cried.

But he just looked back delighted. The turtle dove lower and Stevie fell off into the water. He broke the surface laughing.

"I rode it! I rode it!" he cried. "Did you see?"

"I saw, Stevie."

"It was taking me to Atlantis," he said.

We looked at one another, dumbfounded.

We grabbed each other by the shoulders and spun in a ring. I was delirious, for I thought by saving the turtle, I made amends for the eggs I had crushed. I had evened out things.

That last morning, Stevie stood in the street, violently waving his hand back and forth as we pulled away, and I waved back. He dropped out of sight. We turned onto the causeway.

I turned around in the car. The next morning I flew to Chicago, where Francine and Momma were waiting for me.

THE SUMMER
OF MY
CAPTIVITY

BONJOUR!

Francine had learned French and pretended not to understand a word I was saying. But I did not care. For weeks after we came home, I looked up blinking, surprised to see streets and fields instead of sand and water. I was so happy. I told Francine we had to be nice to each other, but she put her fingers in her ears and cried out, "*Je ne comprends pas!*"

But every time I went to sleep, there was that moment, like evening, passing between. The fireflies sparkled and the storms flashed on our late-night trips to the beach. They rose up in a warm haze of feeling. I had a picture by my bedside of Stevie with his hands on his hips, squinting at the camera. I could almost hear him asking, "Is it OK if I stop smiling?"

But it did not compare with the one that came to me

as I hovered on the edge of sleep—of Stevie, with his head thrown back, surf splashing around him as the turtle dived into the water. *We are joined*, I'd think. *I'm here*, I imagined him answering and then I'd fall asleep. I woke in the morning smiling.

I overwhelmed Francine one day by saying I loved her and wanted to be nice. She laughed in disbelief.

"*Pardonnez-moi?*" she asked.

"I love you."

But she made her fingers into a cross as if she were afraid I was the devil or that she would catch a horrible contagion from me.

At school, she and her friends teased and called me a goody-goody. Only the religious kids tolerated me.

We went back to school in the afternoons or to the church basement, where we prayed for peace and understanding. I didn't like the way they also prayed for *things*, describing them the way game-show announcers described prizes on TV.

They were fun, though. We went for hay rides, went square dancing, and sang Christmas carols in old folks' homes after Thanksgiving. We tested each other on scripture committed to memory. But I didn't participate when they talked about what would happen to the kids who played rock 'n' roll music and listened to Elvis Presley, those who cut them in the halls and wore fancy clothes instead of plain gingham dresses and white socks, black shoes and blue jeans.

"What will happen?" I wanted to know.

"They'll rot in hell," they said. "They'll burn eternally."

"Not Francine," I objected. "She's nice."

But they shook their heads and looked back with pity as they went off in the church bus for more carolling. I looked for Otis, but he had been sent to a home, so there was nobody around. I stayed home reading or lay in bed thinking about summer and Stevie.

I kept trying, but had lost it. I couldn't get the feeling back I had had with Stevie and Uncle Reynaldo and Aunt Violet in the evening; I panicked as other things intervened. The old dreams rose up with jaws to swallow me.

I thought of Glynn in his swimsuit and Jinx, looking so friendly. I tore out pictures from waiting-room magazines. And when I did, I felt guilty.

Others could look at me and know. Francine's friends giggled, and sometimes workmen high up on scaffolding catcalled and whistled and shouted insults as I walked by.

"Faggot," they called, or, "Sissy!"

"Don't panic," I told myself with that same voice I heard narrating atomic bomb fall-out documentaries. "Just head for your nearest shelter."

The only refuge for me, though, was memory, late night reveries, and the calls that came from Charleston. Aunt Violet and Uncle Reynaldo had called nearly every week since my return.

"They sure must have liked you," Momma said proudly.

When no one else listened, I pulled the phone as far away as it reached and asked Aunt Violet, "How is Stevie?"

"He's fine," she'd tell me.

"Tell him hello."

I'd feel as safe and secure as on those stormy nights on the beach when I held him.

I looked forward to going back to Charleston the next summer, but after New Year's they stopped calling. That worried me. We didn't hear from Aunt Violet again until she called one night in February to tell us that the money she had put aside for the N.A.A.C.P. was missing.

"Do you remember where you put it?" Momma

asked, and I could tell by the look on her face that Aunt Violet had snapped at her. I raced upstairs. Listening in on the extension, I heard her say, "I know perfectly well where I put it. I hid it in the library."

I started.

"Hello? Who's there?" she asked. "Is anyone listening?"

I put the phone back and crept down the stairway.

Momma mimed for me to get her a cigarette. "Quick, quick," she mouthed; her hands were so used to the motions they seemed to do it independently. She puffed for a while, but then put it out. She handed the phone to Poppa.

She looked around and asked me into the kitchen and spoke low in case Francine was listening.

"Who's Lula?" she asked.

I told her and Momma looked sad. "Your Aunt Violet says Lula told her she saw you take the money from the library."

I protested. It was as if someone had slapped me. Color rushed to my cheeks.

"Now tell me the truth," Momma said. "Did you take it, honey?"

"No," I said. "I wouldn't take Aunt Violet's money."

Then Poppa came into the kitchen and closed the door. I panicked.

"I didn't do it," I repeated. "It wasn't me." I felt like a trapped bird, my heart beat so violently.

I explained to them about Lula. I told how Aunt Violet and Uncle Reynaldo always took afternoon naps, and it was then that Lula went into the library. She switched on the radio music every day, I said. She had her friends over and made fun of Aunt Violet. "Lula must have taken the money," I told them.

I knew it was true, but even as I said it, I imagined Lula behind bars and I felt guilty.

They called Aunt Violet, but she was not convinced. She said she wanted to talk to me. Trembling, I took the receiver.

"Hello."

"Stop this foolishness," Violet demanded. "Admit you took it. Admit you took the money."

"But I didn't."

Don't you remember? I was thinking. *I was one of you. Remember those nights on the beach? The turtle? Stevie?*

"I saw Lula in the library," I said tentatively.

The line got so quiet that I thought she had hung up. I was going to say, "Aunt Violet?" when suddenly I heard her say, "I'm ashamed of you. A white boy blaming a Negro lady."

"Can I talk to Uncle Reynaldo?" I cried. "He knows what I did in the library!" He would believe me.

But, "He's in bed," she said. "You've made him sick with the whole thing. Let me speak to your mother, boy." Her tones were freezing.

I felt awful, as if I had walked off a cliff. I was falling. With her accusation Aunt Violet had altered the past and in changing my history, had changed me.

"Don't worry," Momma consoled. "Time heals everything. She will have forgotten it all by the time you go see them again."

In April, however, we got word of Uncle Reynaldo's apoplexy—not from Aunt Violet, but from her attorney. I felt unreal, as if in some parallel world these things were happening. It could not be happening to me. It was in Charleston only, that underwater world with Stevie where I used to be. I needed to get back there, to get Aunt Violet to believe me, to get Uncle Reynaldo back into the land of the living.

But boxes came from his estate in the spring: two small cartons of silver dollars for Francine and me. She got some of Reynaldo's mother's jewelry; I got some books from his library. The lawyer suggested someone come down to settle things. It was decided. As soon as school was out, Momma would go to Charleston with me.

A YEAR HAD PASSED, BUT IT
seemed the winking of an eye compared to waiting out
school's last, agonizing weeks. When we finally left, I felt
like a bird that had been freed.

The farther south we drove, the warmer it got.

The land flattened out; we leaned back in our seats.
Instead of moving horizontally, I felt we were falling ver-
tically, passing into time instead of geography.

South Carolina was hazy and dream-like through the
windshield. The air was liquid, the land drowned in heat.
Abandoned houses loomed up in the trees like fantastic
aquarium palaces in seaweed.

We breathed the briny scent of the marshes as we
neared the coast. Our approach was as luxurious as loung-
ing in bed not having to get up, as thrilling as getting hot

before jumping into the sea. "There it is!" Momma cried out.

My heart rose in my throat when I saw Charleston shimmering like haze upon the water. We lost the view from the bridge as we dropped into the streets.

The heat was intense, and I felt the past, like the undertow pulling on me. I wanted to be retrieved, to be taken back, as if the past were a place that existed somewhere physically outside of me. Momma navigated us expertly through the narrow streets.

The house looked just as it had the summer before, hidden behind its high walls covered with vines, waiting. But this time Uncle Reynaldo and Aunt Violet weren't standing on the porch, and it was Momma going up the walk with me.

We rang but no one came.

We called out, then stopped as, like a ghost, Lula materialized behind the dark screen.

I was scared, and Momma tensed beside me.

"How do you do?" Momma said, still maintaining enough of her Charleston upbringing. She expected Lula to obey instantly, but she stayed behind the latched screen eyeing us coolly.

She was wearing one of Aunt Violet's old dresses instead of her old simple gray uniform with the white cuffs she used to wear. She stood in the doorway like the lady of the house.

"Let us in, Lula," Momma said.

"Miss Violet resting," she answered, begrudgingly unlatching the screen.

"Nonsense. She's expecting us. Tell her we're here."

We entered the dark hall and heard Aunt Violet call out from inside the parlor. "Is that them?"

"Yes'm," Lula said, leading us to her.

Aunt Violet had to turn her whole body, and when she saw Momma, she beamed. She had a new set of false teeth that smiled on their own and gave everything she said an air of saccharine insincerity.

Lula stood out in the hall. "Now, Violet, you call if you need me," she said, withdrawing. Later, I saw her sitting in a chair outside the door, peeling an apple, the knife turning in her hand and the peel unfurling.

Aunt Violet nodded after her as foolishly as a schoolgirl with a crush.

After Lula left, Aunt Violet turned to Momma, taking her hand in hers and fussing. She asked about Poppa and Francine without looking at me.

Momma kept trying to bring me up, telling her how well I had done in school and such, but Aunt Violet would have none of it. It made me feel invisible. So after a while I got up and wandered. In the hall, I hesitated.

The house seemed a little shabbier somehow, a little gloomier. It was as if there were less light and less air to breathe.

I opened the door to Reynaldo's library carefully and went in: it was dark. When I opened the shutters, the light that came through seemed not to just pick out objects but to call them into being. Boxes and papers appeared, and I moved through the motes to the paroquet. I reached out to stroke it, but Lula came in and I stopped.

She smiled and picked up an old green vase from the Orient.

"It was in here," she told me.

I nodded, and she put it down and moved through the room as airily as if she were flirting.

"You lose some weight, ain't it?"

I nodded, and she held out her hand, showing off an old silver ring. "Miss Violet give it to me," she said.

"It's pretty."

She agreed. "Miss Violet be a nice lady."

We spoke for a bit and then I went back into the hall. The last time I saw the paroquet, it was locked up with my past in the library.

I DIDN'T TELL MOMMA A
thing. I wanted to leave it all behind me. We drove out to
Sullivan's Island silently. The smells were out. Exhausted
and weighed down, we slept. It was glorious to wake in
the morning. We cleaned.

On the third morning, Momma announced she was
going to town to help Aunt Violet sort through Reynaldo's
belongings to decide which to sell, which to keep, and
which to give to the Historical Society.

"You'll be OK?" she asked.

I nodded. As soon as she pulled out of the driveway,
I went down to the beach to find Stevie.

But he wasn't there, and the tides had erased his gully.
So I went to his side of the island, where, bare of shade,
light pulsed and heat dissolved the edge of things. Shadows
cowered beneath me.

His house was still the same, bowed under its chinaberry trees, but it was like seeing it through fire, wavering in the heat. There were cars up on blocks in the yard, a doorless icebox, and gutted washing machines. I looked on it pleasantly, drowsily as I had back home imagining it just before sleeping.

I listened for a voice or the sound of the TV, but there was only the heat. It made a buzzing sound, a chirring, as if summer itself pulsed out of the earth. It was hypnotizing. I stood thinking and remembering as the heat laid a heavy hand on me.

I looked through the screen and saw all the way through the house to the backyard and made out the vague outlines of things. It was like seeing through time to history.

There, there is where we used to be.

I saw Dulcie in the backyard through a scrim of heat. She seemed in another dimension. Against the mesh of the screen, she was a design of dots as she hung up the wash. I was dazed by the droning heat.

But then I realized, with a cold, prickling fear like an animal's instinct, that someone was watching me.

"Stevie?"

I turned and had to blink against the diffused brightness to make the form become real. I knew who it was in an instant.

Leroy was tousled and unkempt and wore a V-neck T-shirt stained around the armpits. His hands were black with grease and he had a rough growth of beard. I felt his sly animal eyes on me. He hitched up a smile, not friendly but insinuating.

I took in his darkness, his heavy eyes, and his thick arms, tan against his sleeves.

He swaggered up from the car hood. He did not remember my name, yet he knew who I was or knew how— like fumes igniting—he fired me. He smiled and laid the wrench in his hand against his thigh. He stood there but did not say a thing. Our conversation went on without either of us speaking.

"What do you want with Stevie?" he asked finally.

I shrugged, and he laughed.

"Ain't nobody here."

He was lying, and it excited me.

He turned and lay back down on the car hood, lifting his throat to the dappled shade. He slid his hands down his jeans.

I hovered on the steps, intrigued. I knew what he was thinking. I remembered the whispered things, told with giggles, about queers. I wanted to go through with them, to do those things.

Leroy knew it, too. He smiled again and eased to his feet, moving like a fluid.

"Yeah." His voice was warm and sweet as sunlit honey. With his hands in his pockets, he tugged his hips toward me.

"Yeah."

He held my eyes and came toward me, but it felt like *I* was the one moving. I wanted to feel his hands, his arms, his rough beard. I closed my eyes, preparing—not even the siren wailing in the distance bothered me. But I jumped when I heard the screen door slam. Dulcie hollered. "Lee-roy! Lee-roy! Lunch is ready."

He looked at me, probing my eyes, and rubbing his chin. Laughing, he went in to Dulcie.

I DIDN'T KNOW WHAT TO DO
after that. I was frightened and did not go to the beach,
but waited for Momma to come home from the city.

"What did you do today?" she asked.

"Nothing."

She nodded and I leaned against the counter and
listened to her tell about the things she had found in Aunt
Violet's house. She poured them out: pictures of Francine
and me as infants, recipes from the 1850s, and calling cards
and eyeglasses of the deceased.

"That house is a time capsule," she said, laughing.
She swept them up and then started cutting melon and
had me fetch her things.

She had enjoyed herself, getting her work done in the
city. Compared to her, I felt unattached, prey to the feelings
that loomed as high and violent as the purple storm clouds.
Every time I started to speak, thoughts of Leroy intervened.

I was too nervous to go down to Stevie's house the next morning.

That afternoon was freighted with heat and lightning—I came back early from the beach. Glynn and Ivan and Jinx were standing outside the Red and White by the Coke machines. They were bigger, taller, broader than before, Jinx especially. When I recognized them, I hurried by with my eyes down, but they nudged each other and got on their bikes. They swerved near, and Ivan looked back smiling.

"It *is* him," he said.

They biked by the house once or twice as I sat on the porch pretending to read. I watched them surreptitiously. The air was as hot and moist as a mouth on me.

I heard a crack that I supposed was thunder. But there was no lightning, and people ran down the street. A plume of smoke rose up and there was a brown aura of dust in the distance.

"What is it? Where is it coming from?" people were asking. I stood at the edge of the yard and listened.

"Well, I suppose it's nothing."

People started drifting back to their business, but I was worried. Momma did not come in until after six-thirty.

"Did you hear it?" she asked as soon as she drove up with a carload of groceries. I nodded. "What was it?"

A crew digging up the streets had found an old Civil War shell, she said, and it had exploded, collapsing a wall of a building.

"Imagine it still being alive after all these years," Momma said. "Dust was everywhere, into everything. Your Aunt Violet was very upset and wouldn't let Lula leave. Made her spend the night with her. Imagine."

Momma laughed. "That Lula is nice," she told me.

I nodded, but felt uneasy. Looking out into the approaching dark, I thought of what Aunt Violet and Uncle

Reynaldo had told Stevie and me about an old war being waged and how no one had really defeated the enemy. Fireflies could have been the messages sent by guerrillas stealing through the trees. I did not want to go when Momma sent me to the Red and White to buy bread. I ran down the street, dodging a black car that I thought looked like Leroy's. Lurking inside, I waited for it to disappear.

By the time I left the store, lights were coming on in the gas station across the street and a car pulled out of it with a squeal. I looked across to the brightly lit arena, and when I saw who it was at the pumps, I ran. It had to be. It was!

"Stevie," I cried. "It's me."

He was on tiptoes leaning over the hood of a car to reach the windshield. He had his back to me, and he stopped as if shot when he heard his name. He turned around.

His straight-cut bangs hung in his eyes. Freckles spread across his cheeks and his eyes moved closer together as he smiled, deforming his face like a rubber toy being squeezed. He waved and I ran over.

I stood in front of him and for the first time in days felt at ease. I was on firm ground again. We grinned at each other as if we had both just completed a long journey.

"Remember?" I asked.

"Yes."

I hugged him and caught his hand in mine until we stood alongside the car as if we were about to take off in a Virginia reel.

"I've been looking for you!" I said.

"I work here," he answered proudly, and as if to prove it, he turned and lifted the wiper as gently as if it were a bird's wing. With concentration, he moved a squeegee over the windshield.

Another car drove in, making the bell ring—Stevie started toward it with his bucket and squeegee. In his office, Mr. Redmond hoisted himself out of his chair and started our way.

"Can I see you tomorrow?" I asked Stevie.

He smiled and nodded.

"See you in the morning!" I cried.

And he smiled at me.

HE MUST HAVE GONE INTO the kitchen without knocking, for Momma's scream woke me.

By the time I made it in, Stevie was smiling at her quizzically. She had a spatula in her hand and was jabbing it in his direction.

"Stay away!" she said. "Don't you come near me."

"Momma!" I laughed, the way other kids did at me. She swung around in relief. I couldn't believe she didn't understand.

I walked over and took his hand. "It's Stevie," I said. "My friend."

I had to say it again. "My friend Stevie."

She smiled and looked back and forth between us, wrinkling her forehead. Then she laughed insincerely, and put the spatula down. But I could tell she was not pleased.

Back home, she had been head of the committee to get Otis off the streets.

"I'm so sorry," she said lamely. "How are you, Stevie?" she asked with a false, bright smile.

"Fine," he answered, nodding.

Although she usually did not smoke in the mornings, she reached for a pack, took a cigarette out, and lit it. She inhaled deeply, stood back, and looked at us.

"Excuse me," she said. Then she smiled again and ducked out of the kitchen.

Stevie said we should play ball with the kids down the street, but I persuaded him to go to the beach with me. There the old feelings welled up as warmly and as welcoming as the water. We fell back into them and for a long time did not speak—we floated on our backs in two old inner tubes from the gas station. Atlantis rose from the sea.

When we were free, we lay on the sand or in the water, staring at the sky, dipping our arms in to steer. With our chins up, the world was upside down and we laughed at it dizzily. When it was time for me to go home for lunch and for Stevie to go to work, I did not worry. For I knew there would be more mornings; the supply was as endless as the waves that came rolling in to the beach.

"What was your friend's name?" Momma asked that first day when I came back from the shore.

"Stevie."

"Stevie what?"

"Toombs."

"Does he have any family?"

Like her fingers playing across the counter, as on piano keys, so she too was moving—underneath her words, sounding out things.

She stayed home that afternoon and had me help in

that roped-off square of yard that she called a garden. In the evening, I helped her weed.

"Where are you going?" she asked when I finally got up.

"For a walk."

"Do you mind if I come?" she asked, pulling her gloves off and getting off her knees.

"But I'm going to meet somebody," I said.

"Who?" she asked.

"A friend."

She had to know, so I told her.

"Stevie," I said.

She pursed her lips, upset with me.

The light in her room was still on when I came in. She put down the mystery she was reading and asked me if everything was OK.

"Fine," I said.

But she looked worried.

Momma invited Dulcie and Stevie over for supper the next week. Dulcie was flattered, but I was worried. For I knew how polite Momma could be, how she talked down to some ladies. She made them feel welcome while they were there, but when they left, she and Francine would hoot.

"Did you see that dress?"

"That hat!"

"And those horrid earrings!"

I felt disloyal dragging Dulcie in and ignored Momma's winks.

Dulcie and Stevie were dressed up. She wore a heavy green dress that had damp crescents under her arms. She was pale and sweating, wiping her face constantly.

"Are you married?" Momma asked as we ate.

"No, ma'am," Dulcie answered. She put down her fried chicken.

But Momma, after wounding, healed. "Oh, how smart of you," she said, "playing the field."

Dulcie looked up from her plate, gratified and surprised—after that she always spoke of Momma adoringly. So did Stevie. Momma had given him some candy.

That night and the following, I sneaked out of the house without telling Momma. I crept to the gas station to meet Stevie.

We were together whenever he wasn't working. In the mornings we went to the beach, and on Wednesday afternoons when the venue changed, we tramped all the way down to the air-cooled cinema by the fort, arriving hot and sweaty. There we sat in the near-empty darkness, eating stale yellow popcorn, drinking Cokes, and watching Three Stooges movies. We would walk back discussing what we had seen, or I talked and Stevie just listened to me.

After eating supper separately, we met on Middle Street, and sometimes Stevie came back to spend the night with me. We stayed up talking and Momma stayed up reading mysteries—as if we were competing. We raced her into the night and once she turned off her light, we stole out to the beach. There we had those old magic feelings of those stormy evenings.

Days passed pleasantly. I was as complete as the season itself, heavy with happiness and heat. I forgot everything else. Summer would never end, and I would never leave.

July came. The air got thicker; Stevie was slower to move, less apt to speak. When we passed his little friends playing ball in a field, I'd have to pull him along.

"Come on, slowpoke," I'd say. "You don't want to play with them."

But he looked at them as longingly as a thirsty man does at a drink.

One morning he stopped still in front of them, and I asked him, "What is it, Stevie?"

"I want to play ball," he said.

"With them? But who will play with *me?*" He shrugged his shoulders and looked at his feet.

"I know. Let's get some ice cream."

And while we sat eating in the shade of some trees, I asked him about our first summer.

"Remember how you'd ask me questions?"

He nodded.

"We can do it again, Stevie. We can talk about Atlantis. Remember when the turtle tried to take you there?"

"Yes!" he cried delightedly, turning his attention to me.

But he did not show up in the yard the next morning. And when I went looking for him at the gas station, Mr. Redmond said he wasn't working. I found him in the field. I was angry but walked away, pretending not to see.

I lay in wait and ambushed him when he left work that night.

"Going home?" I asked. He nodded and I fell in alongside him.

"I hope you weren't looking for me this morning," I said. "I had to go somewhere."

There was no response.

"The submarine," I added, "was quite interesting."

He looked my way but went on walking.

The next night I ran up to him as he was leaving.

"Guess what?" I cried as if out of breath.

"What?"

"It was wonderful, Stevie! I wish you could have been there. I went to the beach this morning—I went swimming. Deeper and farther out than I have ever been before. And guess what I found? Guess where I went?

"To Atlantis! I made it there. Under the sea, Stevie!"

"You did?" he asked, stopping in the street and cocking his head to one side. He stood still as I walked on. He tugged his pants up and ran after me. He pulled at my sleeve.

"What was it like? How did you get there? Did people walk on the ceiling?"

I laughed and swung deliriously around in a circle. "It was wonderful. Maybe I can take you there one day."

"Yes! Will you? Please?"

"If you keep it secret."

He nodded his head vigorously.

I told him to meet me at the Red and White in the morning, but went instead with Momma to the library in the city.

"Where were you?" he asked that evening.

"I'm sorry," I said. He looked worried.

"I'm not sure I can take you with me, Stevie."

We were walking past the field where the kids were playing.

"If you want me to take you to Atlantis, you can't play with them anymore." I held my breath as he looked back and forth from them to me.

"Why not?" he asked.

I just looked mysterious and walked away. He ran after me.

"Are you sure you went there?"

And I asked him, "What do you think?"

I left him, and the next morning he was waiting for me outside the kitchen door. He followed me around the way he used to, looking at me in awe, half in trepidation that I might disappear.

"Let's go," he urged when we went in the water.

He was in his inner tube paddling out to sea.

"Not now," I told him. I pointed to the shore where some girls were. "They'll see."

"Take me there now!" he demanded. He was angry.

"I can't."

"Tomorrow morning."

"OK," I said, but then I told him it was too stormy.

We went on that way for a few days—him demanding, me demurring, until one evening after sunset I came upon him playing with his friends again.

They were playing a game like dodge ball or keep

away. Stevie had the ball and he held it high over his head, looking for whom to throw it to. He stopped when he saw me.

"Come on," I demanded.

But he shook his head; the kids turned around and scrutinized me.

"I'm going to Atlantis now," I said.

He dropped the ball and came after me.

"Right now?"

"Well—it's probably too dark."

He stopped and stood frozen in the street.

"Stevie," I said. "Please."

His mouth was open, and his arms extended from his sides. I saw the look dawn his eye: incredulity.

"It didn't happen. You didn't go there! You lied!" He was horrified at me. I tried to interrupt, but he stamped his feet.

"You shouldn't lie," he said.

"Don't go, Stevie."

But he did. He ran back to the field. The kids had stopped playing and all turned to look at us.

"Who's he?" they asked.

One boy put his hand on his hip, the other in the air and sashayed around, mimicking me. The others laughed.

I called, "Please."

But Stevie threw the ball and they ran off.

"Baby," I shouted after him, but he did not look back. "I hate you," I screamed. But, "Don't leave," I whispered. "I'm scared." The old panic was back. "Something will get me." I sensed the darkness that lay in the center of summer, like that in the thickening midst of trees, spreading out for me.

"**W**HAT IS IT?" MOMMA ASKED as I moped around that evening. She knelt in the dirt, sticking her hands in, as if it satisfied a need in her.

"Where's Stevie?" she asked.

"Nowhere." I was mad at her for asking and for not instinctively understanding what the matter was and fixing it for me.

"I want to go home," I pouted. "I want to leave."

"Oh, honey," she said. She sat up on her heels like a rabbit and looked at me. "They're only growing pains you're having. You'll have other friends. You'll see."

The light faded, and she went on weeding, moving on her knees. A minute later she called out, saying she had something for me to see. She bent and reached in with her hand and cupped her palm to bring up a blossom as though it were water.

"Passion flower," she said. "See?"

I looked, expecting a voluptuous scarlet-throated thing. I was not impressed with the strange, spiky weed.

"Here are the disciples," she said, pulling back the petals. "The thorns, the cross, the drops of blood." It made me feel like crying, for I wanted everything else to be laid out as clearly and be as full of meaning. Without Stevie, I did not know what was happening.

She led me over to the wooden chairs, and we sat back like astronauts ready for launching. She smoked and pointed out the constellations to me.

We heard the clicking gears of Glynn and his friends' English racers going down the street.

"Who are they?" Momma asked.

"No one."

"But maybe they would like to be your friends. Why don't you try, sweetie?"

I knew they gathered every evening at the empty gas station on Middle Street. It was stuccoed, had Spanish tiles and bracketed eaves—like tourist courts on the side of the road, abandoned in high grass and groves of pecan trees. If I watched them, a sad, silvery feeling like a breeze turning back the leaves came over me.

For something had happened to Glynn and Ivan, to Jinx, Billy, and Lee; something that had not yet happened to me. That summer they seemed more powerful and real, less tentative than they used to be. Each was still himself, only more so somehow. They picked fights with each other, half in earnest, half jocosely. Every evening I watched them leave the old station and fly proudly past me.

Saddened, I'd go sit down. I felt that what Momma called "my growing pains" were not just longings for what I did not have yet, but were yearnings for what I had lost and could no longer be.

Some nights I'd walk the silent island streets looking

for a sign, as if twilight was a gateway between the two worlds. But I could not move from day to night, or life to dreams; dusk was like dust coating my throat, and I could not breathe.

Panicking, I'd go to the garden looking for Momma. But I'd find her on the sofa inside, with the mystery novel she was reading facedown beside her. More often than not, she'd be asleep, with one arm over her eyes and the other flung out above her head, looking like she had been mowed down while fleeing.

"Momma," I'd plead.

Her mouth would open and she'd flip a hand like shooing a fly.

I'd give up and go out, sometimes following Glynn, sometimes Stevie.

Stevie and his friends passed by on their way to vacation Bible school. They filed into the white church in twos, as smugly as onto the ark. Then the other kids biked by. Everyone was saved. Of all the world, only I was lonely.

After Bible lessons, they went to the beach. I followed them. They disintegrated as evening progressed. In the darkness, the boys wearing white shorts and pants streaked.

One evening I watched as Stevie held the ball high above his head. He swayed and the kids followed the way he leaned.

"Give it to me," they pleaded.

"To me, Stevie."

"Here."

"No. Me."

"Me!"

I held out my hand, too. And he smiled.

But then his eyes lit with mischief; he moved in my

direction, but threw it back to another boy, who took off running.

"Here!" they cried.

"Throw it to me!"

"No, me."

It sounded like sea gulls screeching for a piece of bread.

"Me! Me! Me!" they each shrieked.

"Me! Me!"

I could hear that as I walked up the street, as eerie as a banshee's cry, as penetrating as all the calls of history.

I passed the old gas station as Glynn and his friends arrived.

Their faces shone in the dusk the way coals gleam. I paused to watch them and they watched me. They dangled their arms over their handlebars, straddled the seats, and dawdled back and forth on their heels. Green seethed up through the fissures in the concrete as if there were a jungle underneath it. Jinx nudged Glynn's elbow and grinned.

All Glynn wore that summer was a small blue bathing suit that showed off his thighs. He always bent over to pull off whatever shirt he was wearing. His hair was so white it looked like frost, and when he smiled his wide, curved, women's lips, it made me both hot and shivery.

I smiled back.

In the distance, Stevie's friends screamed.

Glynn nodded at me.

We hung there for a while and they stuck their hands deeper in their pockets until Jinx got an idea. He nudged Glynn. And the idea passed among them like electricity. "Want to?" they asked.

They got on their bikes and wheeled away like a flock of pigeons scattering. Only Ivan looked back to see if I was following.

I was. I was running after them, as Stevie's friends continued the cry.

Me. Me. Me.

Soon after this, a bike appeared in the front yard. It was there one morning like a gift from the gods or something washed up on the beach. It was a girl's bike: pink, with a plastic white wicker basket and a banana seat. When no one claimed it, Momma agreed to let me use it.

I had to stand up while I pedaled to keep the handlebars from hitting my knees. But it did not trouble me as I rode those streets with the wind in my ears. It was like sprouting wings. I saw Stevie once, running home like a scared dog when it thundered. I flew by, feeling that I had evolved beyond him. He seemed so juvenile, so silly. I went to the gas station, where the boys were waiting. They got quiet when I appeared.

And when they left, they looked back to see if I was following. I was, but they were faster. They scattered in a different direction every night, but no matter which way they went, they always eventually turned down the island's one last forested street. Just as they neared the corner, they sped up, rose on their pedals, and looked back at me like Orpheus looking back at Eurydice. By the time I got around the bend, they had already disappeared. I rode up and down, looking for where they had vanished, like ghosts, into the green.

The tops of the trees swayed like seaweed, and the light that filtered through was eerie. I stopped at the trash pile at the end of the street, where a sofa spewed its stuffing. Lying nearby was a plastic doll whose one blue eye had powdered to white; half its yellow hair was ripped out. The rest of it stood straight up and its mouth puckered in a scream.

I peered into the woods. I knew they had to be nearby. I crept in and came upon an old set of gates. They just seemed to materialize. Light and shade spun and a dizzying déjà vu came over me.

We had stopped in front of them last summer, Uncle Reynaldo, Stevie, and I. Down there, he said, was a cemetery. I walked on quietly and sure enough, a narrow path led to a clearing. I approached cautiously and saw a few tombstones; those that had not fallen slanted at odd angles. Some leaned on each other drunkenly. The dark, splintered remains of others stood like runes among the saplings.

I listened.

The air was watery and I could not read any of the names; they were filled in by twigs and leaves. I reached out to brush away some of the debris so I could read the lettering, but I stopped. It had gotten too quiet suddenly. I thought of how it could be, like the roll call on judgment day, if I said the name aloud and there came an answering "Here."

I tried to find Stevie that night, but he was off with his friends. And the night after that was when the others came for me.

I WAS LYING ON MY BED after supper. Momma was doing dishes. She stopped and then she said in that voice she used when she showed me a rainbow or a sunset, "Honey, come here." I came quickly.

She was staring out the window at their silhouettes as they stood in a half ring. We went out to the porch and Glynn and Jinx and the rest motioned for me.

I was scared, but Momma said, "Go on." She nodded at the boys and then kissed me. "See? I told you things would get better." She pushed me gently to the stairs. "Go on, sweetie."

I got on my bike and they led me down the street, past Stevie—who looked up like I was Elijah going on to glory—past the stores, past everything, as if we were rising off the streets. The locusts were a pulse in my ear.

Then they sped off, leaving Lee behind as a guide. He stood in front of the cemetery gates, almost waist-high in the green. He made sure I was following.

He led me into the trees.

We hit bumps, and the fenders of our bikes stuttered against the wheels as flashes of the boys' shirts darted like tropical birds in the green. We came to the verge of another clearing.

Then they laid down their bikes and slipped past a series of long, low cement structures that had once been painted black, but from time and mildew and the sea had been stained green. It was just as Reynaldo had said it would be, as if I could hear him speaking—the old quarantine station looked like Angkor Wat, an ancient remnant of a jungle civilization forgotten for centuries. Doors opened down corridors lost in dreams. In the half-light I could read the old numbers of the rooms and signs that read, "QUARANTINE."

I wanted to stop, to stare, to take it all in, but the boys kept on going. They went toward a rectangular wooden building that had slipped off its piers so it leaned two ways simultaneously. As they climbed in the windows, it suddenly looked like an insect on its back with all legs wiggling.

I was alone then. Insects rasped in the trees; the shadows lengthened, tipping us toward evening. Mosquitoes rose and I itched, a crucifix pierced at ankles and wrists. As I moved forward, the green seemed to rise out of the leaves and tinge the atmosphere. Closer still, I laid my cheek against the silvered, paintless side of the building as if to the cool flanks of a huge, fallen beast. I put my ear to it, listening as if for a heartbeat.

Finally.

I fell back as Jinx came around the corner. His shirt was off, his chest polished as driftwood.

He pointed and I followed him as he swung himself

up through the tilting doorway and held his hand out for me. He pulled and I scrambled up after him. Day was dissolving. I held on to the jambs and could just barely see. Inside, the boys were blurs, hanging in the dimness like huge white moths. I crossed over, the slanted floor pulling at me.

In a tableau of gray and white, the boys were in their underpants, just as in the magazine. I moved cautiously.

Smiling, Jinx slid his underwear off, kicking it into a corner. Billy folded his like a flag. They all began to move in, ringing me, and I looked around joyously as the old abandoned visions flooded back to life. They all came forward, while Ivan hung back, holding his hands in front of him. He shook his head back and forth slowly.

"No, don't do it," he shouted. He was crying.

I was coming forward, too, but Glynn broke through like something buoyant rising from the deep. He moved in a slow strut, his smile growing as he reached out. I brushed him with my eyes. He pushed me to my knees. All I was aware of then was a small scar on his hip, worm-like and curling. That . . . and Ivan's tears. The other boys closed in around me.

"Queer," Glynn said derisively.

It rose in a chant, like the wind, like the years. They shouted it like it was an insult, but it was music to my ears. Glynn tipped me up by my chin so when I looked up, I saw a colossus. And as soon as he was sure I saw his contempt, as soon as he saw my surrender, he let my head down.

He let me.

Then it was Billy's turn. But Jinx broke in. So did Lee. "Me," they shouted. Each wanted to be next.

Ivan tried to keep them away; he tried to interpose

himself. They flung him off and came up to me. I gave him a pitying smile, and to the boys I gave in as if to the sea.

"One at a time," I said, and they obeyed.

That was it: the way out of summer, to here.

PART
3

IT
WAS LIKE
GARDENS

It TOOK YEARS TO MAKE IT back here—but they passed swiftly enough.

The door opened and I went through, not knowing where I was going. It's hard to believe—these afternoons here—that I did not see. But I went along, paying attention to the thread of events, ignoring the pattern and weave.

As I got older, I gave a name to what I was doing. I told myself I was looking for love, and each face I collected removed me just a jot more from that sad little boy I had been with Stevie. I broke with myself and him completely, and was disdainful even of the memory. It was ballast, the past dragging on me.

I felt it was banished when I woke up in that quarantine hut. So were the boys. All but Jinx. He came back for another helping. When he was gone, I went past the abandoned old buildings, feeling outside myself, already escaped to the future, bringing on my destiny, as if I could see them all—those whom I would meet.

And once I left, I saw others going in the same direction—the guys, who in ghostly battalion, would parallel and precede me here. I found others who believed.

We dreamed the same thing as if mass produced, as if one size fit all, come from K-Mart or Sears. It rose up and we followed. In its thrall, I left the city.

But not for a few weeks yet. Once summer burned out, Momma and I left the beach.

So the boys and I had a series of evenings to pursue our couplings. Days did not matter—they were preparations only. Only the moments we convened together were real. All but Ivan called again and again for me.

He tried desperately to keep them out of my power, but couldn't. I ignored him when he came up to me one day and put his face in mine. Eye to eye, he said he was going to get me. But I knew he couldn't. No more than his friends could stop coming. Jinx especially seemed crazy around me.

They grew afraid of my power, I think, and were relieved when it came time for Momma and me to leave. The beach house was sold. And Reynaldo's things were taken to the Historical Society.

So Momma said good-bye to Lula and Aunt Violet.

I even drove a little. I kept my eyes on the road, to where it would take me. Momma talked on and on about how my new friends had matured me.

For a year I did nothing, keeping to myself, imagining how it would be. But in high school, word got out and boys would whisper in the halls, "We have a car."

At night, Francine's boyfriend would call me.

After school I'd choose, and the losers would pile dejectedly into their car and speed off, looking back through their rear window as the winning car drew up. I'd get in and the boys would get quiet. We'd drive along roads swamped in greenery, too excited to speak. We'd go out into the woods; with the towel we brought along it must have looked like we were picnicking.

But when I'd get on the towel, the boys' voices would get high and quavery. Their voices would break when they'd ask, "Is it OK? Does it hurt?"

Some boys were scared while others were sweet. The ones I liked most were those who took it for granted, those who almost got as much pleasure denying themselves to me as they did giving in.

I kept looking as the years advanced. I went off to college. Outside feelings like spring, morning, holidays, or evenings had no influence on me anymore. Like a virus, the dream, the idea, was inside me. I could sense *him*—whoever my lover would be—somewhere, waiting. He pulled on me like the moon pulled on the sea, like gravity. I could feel his mass, could hear his voice, could imagine him next to me.

I thought he was near the night I saw a blond boy walk down the street and disappear through a heavy metal door that was always padlocked in the morning. The building had an old theater marquee on which fabulous names like Baby Doll Latour and Voluptua Muldoone appeared. I went through the door and entered a space that I had thought existed only inside me. All I was aware of at the end of the narrow hall were eyes in the darkness, like stars swirling down around me.

I went through the blackout curtains up to the bar, and men with their backs to the entrance turned around to look at me. It was like gardens—their flowers turned toward the sun, twisting with desire, deformed with need. So it was with them, with me. That night they turned to see if I was the one they were expecting.

I went up to the bar, and just as another man was

coming over, the blond boy slid me a beer. I smiled but kept my eyes down. He lifted my chin. Everything he said sounded like something I had heard before, and that comforted me.

He took me to his apartment that night, and unlike the kids in high school who after our encounters would flee without a word and avoid me in the hall for weeks, he talked and even kissed me. I thought I was in love, that Barry—that's what he said his name was—would complete me.

But he was to be just a stepping-stone. Barry's is one of the faces I see as afternoons melt into evenings. The faces fly past like swifts out of chimneys.

When I went back to the bar the next night, Barry looked at me as if he had never seen me before, or worse, as if he were angry. And he was, for I moodily watched him all evening.

"Don't you remember?" I wanted to say. I watched him tell people his name was Lloyd and then leave with a boy, one better-looking than me. Behind the bar was a mirror and in it I saw myself: the desperate face of the one I used to be. It was like the night on the beach that Momma explained the passion flower. I saw it all laid out and explained. I had to escape from myself, from being lonely. I had to get others.

So I turned away from my face and looked around the bar. There was a group of men sitting on bar stools grinning my way. One got up and motioned me over, patting his empty seat. I sat down, and he put his hand on my arm. Another bought me a beer.

They took me to a hotel room and undressed me.

Norman patted my temples and soothed my brow. He took my glasses off and folded them. He whispered as the others lifted and spread, like he was attending me. I was alone with Norman after the others went to sleep. His face comes up, too, these evenings. I can see his graying hair and massive chest, then sinking with age. I felt another dimension with him, like he was a temple or Ozymandius, his flesh smoothed by past victories. When he was done, he cradled me in his arms and whispered things.

I stayed with Norman through my senior year even though he smoked too much and his beard scratched me. I stayed until my feelings for him chafed on me like a collar and nagged like an obligation. There were others out there, I knew, but the college I went to offered few opportunities.

For several years I waited and looked, sure that any minute it would happen for me.

I went off to graduate school and did well in history. I took my studies seriously. But as evening came on, I was restless. It was only then, when I was looking for love, that I was real. It was my true calling. I walked the streets, feeling as I had with Stevie on the beach, a ghost outside my body.

Any door to any bar I opened admitted me. Outside, I had a secret identity, like a Jew in the Inquisition, posing like a Marano, a false convert to Christianity. Inside, however, I was free to breathe. I could indulge in the secret rituals that others outside called heresy.

Nights could be heaven, as they had been on the beach. If one did not reach for the beauties, others would get them instead. All of us in the bars knew this. Our dreams were our duty. If I did not get what I felt I deserved, the only one to blame was me. Life then was charged with the imminence of love as the air on the island had been with electricity. I'd see a handsome man and if he asked me to dance, *Nothing else matters*, I would think. *These are the moments that are me.*

The dance always ended, and even if he went home without me, I knew it was not over. The man I was looking for might come out the next evening. He was real. He had to be; for I had glimpsed him in bars and seen him in magazines. I had felt the brush of his wings and had looked into his eyes as he swept up the fellow next to me. If it existed for others, it had to exist for me.

As I moved from job to job, city to city, I thought so many things were happening. But it was the same old thing, repeatedly.

I lived in California and New York. Then I went to Boston. The place I went to there was the park by the river, the Fenway. I went there to look when I was lonely, or when something troubled me. I went there when I heard of Aunt Violet's death. The water and the weeds reminded me of the marshes by Sullivan's Island, and for the first time in years, memory, like remorse, washed over me and I re-membered Stevie.

I was just sitting there, watching men looking for other men wander in the maze of green, like damned creatures in a Heironymus Bosch painting. A man sat on the back of a bench with his chin on his hands and his elbows on his knees. He looked like a child and he looked at me.

That was Bartholomew. He had shiny blond hair, a boy's smile and was bottom-heavy.

"You're not going in there?" he asked in mock horror as I got up and moved toward the dense area by the river. I looked down the path, but he looked me in the eye. I didn't see it then or for years afterward, but I do now. He reminded me of Stevie.

Bartholomew's face comes up in my memory with the others, a perfect succession like that of the kings and queens of England, or my own genealogy.

We were friends until I left Boston, but we never lived together. Bartholomew's apartment was near the stadium, and in the summer we could hear the cheers as we lay in bed and waved our cigarettes around like actresses in bad movies. But Bart's gentleness, the reverence with which he touched me, began to cloy.

We tried to make it work, but it did not. I wanted the stories I read in magazines, wanted to live the ghost images that haunted me. I'd go to the gym and see the hard bodies. The boys in the bars told me stories, and I felt cheated that they had not happened to me. I wanted those big, rough men as crude as drawings. Bart's love smothered. I felt like a fish in a pond with the water drying up around me. When his face comes up these nights, it is just as it was then—mute with pleading. I had to leave.

I wandered for a few months, looking for the dream. I was in my late twenties and love had not come to me. Yet I felt its possibility just as much as before, barely out of reach, tantalizingly near. I was desperate, wondering.

I was offered a job in Savannah and was not going to take it, but by then rumors had popped up, and newspaper articles had appeared. Men in cities were starting to get sick; purple blotches like storm clouds were appearing on faces and arms and bodies. There was a strange new disease. I wanted to flee.

A position came open in Charleston at the Historical Society. I took it impulsively.

I sometimes felt sad as I walked the familiar, old streets, but at other times I remembered Glynn and Ivan and the rest of them in the old quarantine hut. I thought I saw someone who looked like Jinx looking at me. I sensed *Him* just about to reach.

It was easy. I just relaxed and gave into the past and to history, hoping the saturation point would be reached and that dreams would crystalize, condense and come out of their solution for me. It was like being on land yet feeling the pull of the sea.

Those years in between leaving and returning blur now. All is soft in-between, like Brie. Like the afternoons here, things fade out and then come back with a start: how can night be nigh, I wonder, how can it almost be evening? Time that I cannot account for has been lost.

Yet time has not changed in the city.

IT WAS SUMMER WHEN I
returned to Charleston: as if it had stayed that way since
I left. The streets writhed with heat; skies were glazed, and
colors were absorbed into the walls of buildings until evening gave them off luminously. The city seemed immersed
in herself. She did not need the people who passed in her
streets, existing for herself only.

I found two gay bars, and men gathered by the water
in the park called the battery. I was compelled to go there,
as if looking for my kind who would know me. As I walked
down the streets I felt something attached to me, an *other*,
a history, slinking alongside me. If I looked in the windows
I knew I would see more than a reflection, I'd see a view
to a parallel world where events transpired to lure me.

On King Street, I passed stores whose windows were
fly-specked and empty. Mannequins with no arms stood
by like Greek statues, witnessing. On an impulse I went

by Woolworth's to see if Dulcie could still be working there, and it was there that I got the first sense that Charleston had not changed at all. I had come back to a place that was waiting for me.

Dulcie had put on weight, so much so that she walked like a duck. But she still wore her hair shoulder-length and her face was still soft and sweet. Her pale eyes, squinting behind her colorless oval glasses, gave her a puzzled look, as if something had just gone by and she had missed it. I wondered if I should have spoken, for she had not recognized me at first. I could have gotten off scot-free.

But I told her who I was, and her eyes lit up; she seemed glad to see me.

"How's Stevie?" I asked.

"He's fine," she said. "Come on out and see."

So I returned that night in my car to take her to the beach. It was raining, and Dulcie was standing under the awning as lights began to shine off the slick street. She was enormous in her green poncho. With her hood up and face sticking out, she looked like a seal. When I stopped, she handed her bags in and hoisted her legs into place like dead weights. She sighed in the air conditioning.

For a good while she said nothing, but then began talking about Stevie. The way she spoke of him reminded me of Eskimos and all their words for snow, so familiar was Dulcie with all the gradations and peculiarities of her brother. Stevie was her expertise.

As I listened, I found myself getting nervous. Like a cripple going to Lourdes or something, I too wanted healing. She explained his day for me, that he would be home napping.

"He stuffs envelopes at the Hope Center," she said. "The bus comes and gets him and brings him back in the evening. The director's a colored lady," she said a second later. She looked my way quickly to see what kind of effect it would have. I didn't say a thing, and neither did she. "But she's nice," she added finally.

We turned down her street. The yard was still filled with rusting car hulks now covered with vines. I thought about Leroy and looked at Dulcie's fingers. I didn't say a thing. The rings she wore were of Woolworth's quality.

I stopped the car and we got out into the heat, moving slowly, like decompressing. Our glasses steamed; water dripped from the skies and trees. She unlocked the door and held open the screen for me and as I went in, it was like those evenings long ago when storms woke Stevie and me. Suddenly, I was in a warm special place. I almost felt giddy.

I watched Dulcie pull off her poncho and ease out of her thick-soled shoes. She sighed deeply, gave her limp hair a squeeze, and peered into the living room. Everything was as I remembered it. But there was no Stevie. She padded down the hall to an open door and motioned.

"Here."

She waved me over as if tempting me to come upon something I had been searching for. I came up eagerly.

Stevie had just woken from his nap. He was in the middle of the bed in a tumble of sheets he had just erupted from. His hair, rusty at the edges, stuck up. He rapidly blinked his close-set eyes. The sad little retarded man with a big stomach had the expressions of a child. His eyes and face were Stevie's.

He got up slowly, leaning forward some, his arms drooping, his face happy yet concentrating. He seemed to have stalled between boy and man and was caught in the sad twilight of in-between, the way I felt I used to be. But the knowledge that I had made it through was freeing, and because he had brought me this realization, I looked at Stevie tenderly. I cried out his name.

He looked up eagerly. Dulcie straightened his hair as

I sat down on the bed. He looked away shyly, assuming that I could not see him if he could not see me.

"Oh, Stevie," Dulcie chided. "Don't you remember?"

He shook his head.

"No?"

Again he shook his head.

"You sure?" She sat down next to him on the bed and side by side, I sensed something pass between them. She smiled and said, "You remember now, don't you?"

Stevie nodded happily.

"Yes!" Dulcie said, then got up. "Stay for supper," she called to me from the hallway. I heard her turn on the TV.

Alone together, Stevie looked at me and I looked at him and saw that youth had not left his face as much as it had withered in place.

"I'm glad to see you again," I told him.

He smiled like he didn't understand me. He got up and went into the kitchen, shuffling past me in his slippers, hunched over with his hands almost hitting his knees like a monkey. I found him sitting on a stool by the counter, watching Dulcie fry chicken. The heat in the kitchen was intense, as if the air were the bubbling grease itself. But Stevie and Dulcie were happy, and I was, too.

Without me saying a thing, Dulcie took a beer from the refrigerator, popped its top, and handed it over. I drank it on the porch while watching the rain and looking over the cars until supper was ready.

She brought in a fan and we sat in its dull roar as we ate. Stevie grew more animated and gyrated in his seat, but suddenly he cocked his head as if listening. He stretched his face toward Dulcie.

"Still scared of storms?" I asked, hearing the thunder roll in the distance. "Remember how we used to hold each other?"

He looked at me as if I were reading his mind. Then he smiled.

"You were great friends, together all the time," Dulcie encouraged. Stevie smiled, showing gums and teeth, and I felt relief. He remembered me. It was snug in there. I wanted to hug him.

While Dulcie washed the dishes, I sat with Stevie. I tried to play cards with him, but he just wanted to watch TV. He asked me a few questions, and then Dulcie came in and picked up a magazine. She looked at me and I asked, "Yes?" but she looked down quickly.

Throughout that hot, damp evening, as Stevie and I played—I got him to play battle—she looked back as if she wanted to speak, but never did. We smiled at each other every time our eyes met. Later, she folded her hands over her protruding stomach like a pregnant lady.

The rain continued in driblets. The clock ticked. Frogs croaked loudly. The heaviness in there sank around us, encasing us like insects in amber. I myself was nodding off when Dulcie got out of her chair at ten-thirty and heaved Stevie still dozing out of his. She put her arms under him and walked him down the hall as if he were a puppet. I got up to stretch and heard him brushing his teeth.

She came back with a glass of iced tea and a piece of cake. She watched me eat, satisfied as Momma used to be when I came home from college. I remembered how she would stay up late, talking, trying to catch up with me and gauge the changes, looking me over proudly. I felt the most grown-up and glorious then, just as I did now with Dulcie. But the way she kept looking shyly up at me made me feel she was expecting more. I had the maddening sense I had forgotten something and that she was trying to remind me. It was only as I was leaving that I remembered.

"Where's Leroy?" I asked.

"He's married," she said, putting her hands together.

"Oh." I tried to change the subject, but she clung to it.

"He's got some kids. Youngest's named Stevie."

"That's nice."

"His wife's gone, though. He wrote to tell." Dulcie looked down the hall to see if anyone—namely Stevie—was listening. "I think he misses me," she said in a low voice that broke. She smiled helplessly and I smiled back, but she must have thought I was making fun of her.

"He does!" she said. "Really! He needs someone to take care of his babies. I'll show you. He writes me."

"Dulcie," I cried out. "You don't have to show me anything."

But by then she was back with a pack of letters splayed out in her hand.

"See?" she said, holding them out like a card trick, waiting for me to pick one. I saw all of the addresses were in Tennessee. "He wants me to visit," she said.

"And I think you should."

"You do?" she asked. I wondered if it was the wrong thing to say, for suddenly she stopped as if struck; she was about to take the letters back but now turned around to face me. The room had gotten quiet.

"You think I should visit?"

I nodded.

"Stevie didn't think so," she started slowly, but then warmed to the subject. "I would like to. I've been saving. I have the money." She looked up into my eyes and I realized she was looking for someone to lead her.

"I definitely think you should go," I said wisely. "Tennessee is not that far. It would be good for you, Dulcie." She looked at me in awe, as if I were Solomon.

I put down the empty glass and made to leave. She followed me to the door like a dog, hanging on, enchanted, to my every word. I felt as if I had just walked through a big spider web; the same clinging feeling made me wince and want to brush free.

By the time I was at my car, I was already looking back. Dulcie had her head out the door watching me. I waved.

I thought of Stevie and her as I drove back to town, where the old sorrows still drizzled in the streets. Futility shone off the windows. But I was happy.

I**T MUST HAVE HAD SOME-**thing to do with summer and me not knowing anybody. I went back there after work and on weekends, and they deferred to me. It was like one of the unreal dreams that come after tragedies—someone has died or something awful has happened and you dream that your friend is really alive, but maybe just can't do as much; or everybody else has to think them dead, but you are special and are allowed to visit. I'd feel that same strange inner elation in me as I'd drive out to the beach.

I'd visit, sit, and watch TV with them, and sometimes when Dulcie was too tired, I'd go into the bathroom to supervise Stevie in the tub. Often he was cranky and wept bitterly. But at other times he'd laugh and splash and I'd dry him off and we'd settle down and watch a movie.

When I left, I'd end up at the bar every now and then, but more often than not, I just went home, thinking about the evening, feeling warm inside, as if I had done something important. Time spent in the bar was no longer satisfying, but I stopped there just often enough to not lose touch with what was happening.

I knew some younger kids who lived on the same court I did. They—Talbert and Jerry—had helped me move in. After unpacking, they had stood around looking at my things the same way I used to stare at Poppa after his trips to see if he had brought me anything. But I felt I had let them down, not having any glamour left from the far-off places I had been. They took me to the bar that night, and when I went there afterwards I sat with them and their friends Harris and Lannoo and their fat friend Tiny, who shrieked grandly at everything. Lannoo was the best-looking, so only he could go sit with the handsome men who lounged along the banquettes apart from the rest of us, watching who entered to decide who was deserving of being elevated into their company.

Everywhere I had been, I encountered them, these aristocrats of beauty, not a one of whom would condescend to me. Everyone in the bar watched their movements and speculated about their love affairs, following them as housewives would soap opera stars or Greeks would their deities. "Me, me, me," we'd each plead silently as they scanned the dance floor.

But I gave up on them after I started seeing Stevie and Dulcie.

We did tourist things—went to the plantations out of town, to the museum, and to the movies. Summer settled into a routine, swinging slowly like a pendulum from nights on the beach to days at the Historical Society. At work, re-searchers stared at us as if suspecting us of having doctored the records and supposing that if they took their eyes off us, we would alter history. After work, I'd go home and sleep.

When I woke up, the world would be changing. In the courtyard, shadows stretched and elongated like cats after napping. I went down the steps to the rusted cast-iron fountain and fed the swollen goldfish. Shutters opened on the upper floors as people leaned out. Darkness brought coolness and relief, and I felt somehow that I had gone down with the day and lost my identity. Talbert and Jerry would come out and talk with their friends. Their words came as easily as the fountain's splashing, and were as meaningless. Occasionally I lingered and had a drink, listening to what happened in the bar and which men they wanted to meet.

It was sad, listening to them. For like things defined by their antithesis, as life by death and wisdom by stupidity, their dreams, in obverse, told their histories. One night they even asked about me, and, looking back over my past, I saw it was like stepping off a plank into the sea. I thought of Glynn and Jinx and the house in the trees. All the faces I had collected came back, and for the first time they scared me. Why were they going on into history with me?

I got up, panicked, but I told them, "Oh, not much ever happened to me." I was sad all evening.

Only when I got to the beach did I feel relief. I spent the nights with Stevie.

I now was only happy with them, and that was why the whole thing with Ricky was so surprising. For I was not really looking for anybody.

Yet I participated in the rites of the city. I accepted invitations from old friends of Momma's, just to be doing something. Teetering old ladies reached out to grab me as if the floors of their old houses were slanted.

"Oh, we'll fix you up," they said. "Won't we?" They sent their husbands, silent and sad as spaniels, off to mix the drinks.

They were friendly, but they were so old, so weathered. Wearing makeup and sweating, they seemed like melting waxwork figures. When they touched their faces, they took back flesh-colored hankies. I winced when they referred to nigras and queers, even though many of their husbands after too much to drink would end up at the battery. Late at night, as we listened to cars pass and to the ice melt in our drinks, we talked on about the city, not only as if Charleston were a living thing but as if it could hear.

It was on one of these evenings that I met Ricky Dandridge at a dinner party. He said he owned an antique shop on Queen Street called Her Majesty's. Other than that, he did not say another word to me, although every now and then I caught him looking my way. He had blondish hair, wore small tortoise-shell glasses whose glare hid his eyes, and his smile showed ragged teeth. Slightly plump, and most precise in his pronunciation, he was a great favorite with the old ladies, who laughed and cried out, scandalized, "Oh, Ricky!" He seemed interested that I worked at the Historical Society.

The next night, just as I was leaving my apartment for the beach, he appeared. He was combing his damp yellow hair when I opened the door. He quickly put the comb into his pocket and flashed his teeth. The violet in his madras jacket trembled like the shadows under his eyes.

"Going somewhere?" he asked brightly.

"Oh no," I lied. "Just to the store for something. Come on in."

In the kitchen, I phoned Dulcie and told her I was not coming out. "Another time," I told her.

"Sure," she said, not worried.

In the living room, I found Ricky looking at my things. I tried to explain their significance to me, but he was not really listening. He put a framed photo of my family down and shifted his curious gaze my way. He laughed brilliantly, but in our silences, he seemed to be weighing things. Pros and cons, no doubt. He left after finishing his drink, thoroughly puzzling me.

After washing the glasses, I was ready to phone Dulcie again. But Ricky called. Did I want to go to a party on Friday? He'd pick me up about seven-thirty.

———

The doorbell and the bells of St. Michael's rang simultaneously.

We went out to the courtyard. Talbert and Jerry and Tiny were sitting around the fountain. I wanted to introduce them, but Ricky tugged at me as if he had a gun to my side.

"Let's just keep on walking," he said as he pulled me along, yet he cheerily waved at them. "I'll go get the car."

For some reason he had parked way down the street.

Once we were inside, he told me confidentially that he was from Virginia, not Charleston. He told me this as if it were a kindness, tipping me off as to the fact of his royalty. He had only been in town for five years and had spent the last three at Her Majesty's, but if I wanted to know *anything*, he said, patting my knees, about *anybody*, "You ask me." He knew, he assured me, not only who was who, but who had what in each attic and closet and family.

As we pulled away, he looked into the rearview mirror as cautiously as a secret agent with a double identity. He kept two different address books, he told me, and whenever any of his straight and gay friends met, he switched into high gear and launched into an act of bravado, like the attack stance of a creature whose hiding place is revealed. He presented me to his straight friends and them to me as if we had been dying to meet. He brought people together dramatically as cymbals clashing, and in the confusion no one really got to talk or learn anything about anybody else or ask a question such as, "And how do you know Ricky?" He felt he had to be straight, not just for his family and his business, but for his position in society.

"But you know how it is," he said. He tapped my knee and gave me a wink. I was amazed to discover that he was three years younger than me.

I did not speak as we drove along. When I finally

asked where we were going, I was confused. "Turn there,"
I said, but he looked at me sharply.

He took a circuitous route, parking way down Water
Street. We sneaked down an alley to the back garden gate
of a house on East Bay. We crunched on a cinder path as
the moon pricked the darkness around us and he opened
an unlatched door.

"Do you live here?" I asked.

"No," he said. "A friend does—with his parents. But
they're out of town. Everyone's upstairs in the air conditioning."

We passed through the kitchen, Ricky pushing me on
as quick as a thief into the dining room, up a ghostly
staircase, through a white paneled door, and into the cool
second-floor library. Maybe it was circling through the
streets, stealing through the dark rooms beneath with their
heirlooms and antiques covered in sheets, and then emerg-
ing into the light, but when Ricky threw open the library
door and the men in there looked up, I was dazzled and
I blinked. I was dizzy, for it was like being thrust into the
holy of holies; if not beauties, I was at least in the presence
of the cream of Charleston gay society. They looked up as
guiltily as if we had interrupted an orgy, but when they
saw Ricky, they relaxed. A TV was on and entranced in
its thrall was a circle of transfixed men.

Ricky introduced me to Seabrook, Van, Rutledge, and
Nowell Pinckney. As each was introduced, he rose off the
white sofa and extended his hand and looked at me as if
I had entered a bar. Van looked at me intently.

Like Ricky, they all led double lives. To protect their
names, they never would be caught dead at the battery.

So it was as if they were in hiding. From their high-
ceilinged rooms and framed family trees, they looked down
upon those who had the nerve to think Charleston was
their city. The men I met up there felt they and their
families owned Charleston exclusively.

Seabrook, the host, was tall and thin and had a handsome, elongated face like a gentleman in an El Greco painting. He fetched a gin and tonic and handed it over with a cocktail napkin as Ricky stood back to gauge the effect all this wealth had on me. Suddenly, as I looked at Van and he started, I felt uneasy, as if he saw through me; but then Seabrook pressed the button on the VCR and we all turned to watch *All About Eve*.

I sat back as they pretended to relax, but all cast glances my way, Van especially. He was puzzled by something and I saw that he solved it: a light came to his eyes and he smiled suddenly. I excused myself, and when I came back from the bathroom—you had to go back out into the hot, dark house to the end of a long hallway— Ricky was saying, "What do you think?" I did not ask about what, because I knew they had been talking about me.

Van winked.

After the movie, we drank pitchers of Long Island iced tea. Ricky moved in closer and put his damp hand over mine. I smiled at him and he patted me. The idea of sex was everywhere, but civility was maintained on the white sofa; so much so it was exhausting. The hours unrolled—we could hear St. Michael's bells and would comment occasionally on them. One by one, we dropped off to sleep.

Just before I went under, Ricky said that the colors would never go together. "Plum and puce," he said. "See?"

I jumped when he woke us just before dawn.

"Up, up, my beauties!"

We rose, looking around us as if we had lost something. Then everyone scattered down the alley.

Later in the day, we regrouped at the beach. Rutledge's parents had a house on Sullivan's Island, where we showered after swimming; we had watermelon with his family. His mother said she remembered mine.

"You tell her Betsy Beaufort says hello," she said warmly, and showed me a picture of the two of them at Ashley Hall.

Ricky beamed.

I got up and looked at the other black-and-white photos along the wall. Some faces looked familiar—too familiar. I was sweating.

"What is it?" Ricky whispered.

"It's just the heat," I lied. "Who's he?" I asked Rutledge, pointing.

"My cousin Glynn. Do you know him?" He was excited. "He and his wife are coming out this evening."

"We used to play together," Van said, smiling.

Fortunately, we left soon after. Seabrook and Rutledge and his sister went to a movie and Van was doing something with his family. Ricky invited me to his apartment for supper. He talked on and on as if we were best friends or intimates already, talking about what we would do together. He said that after supper he was going to seduce me. He laughed lavishly.

We were finishing our coffee out on his narrow little shuttered porch. Over rooftops sunset gilded the city. Talk gave out; he looked at his watch, put his cigarette out, reached out his hand, and put his mouth over mine. His glasses were smudged and his face was greasy. He was weaving slightly.

He went in and flung open the French doors to his bedroom. He showed me an elegant rice bed. "On loan," he said, "from Her Majesty's!" We undressed and lay in it amid the drapes and canopies, as unmoved as an effigy.

He was diligent, but like his bed, wooden. When he was done, he lay back in his silk robe and sighed deeply as if he had rarely been so gratified. He got up to shower, leaving me feeling frustrated.

When he came back in his silver and blue pajamas, he sat down cross-legged in the bed and talked more of the fabulous things we would do and the shops to which he would take me. I said nothing. He ground out his cigarette in a tiny hand-held ashtray and kept looking at me. He started to talk about his landlady.

"Oh," I said, jumping up, finally realizing he wanted me to leave. "I'm sorry." Once I was dressed again, he inspected me and hung back behind the door.

Growing brave, he stuck his head out and blew me a kiss as I slipped down the hallway.

THE PHONE RANG AT NOON.

"I didn't see you at church," he said. "Shame on you! Let's go bike riding."

So we did. He careened grandly on his blue bicycle and rang his bell at everybody.

Later that afternoon, we went to a garden party where men in white played croquet. He kept calling, and because summer was picking up the city and tilting it until the streets were nearly empty, and because I sensed what he could do for me, I kept going. It was easier to give in to Ricky than to resist him.

It was because he hammered at me all the time. Sometimes, though, I genuinely liked him, when I saw through to what was beneath, the way he saw through nicks, varnishes, and years of abuse to a true antique. Maybe he, too, was worth salvaging.

But it was so difficult. I tried not to admit it, but Ricky never seemed comfortable when he was alone with me. I was a stand-in for somebody. Only when he was with his friends was he at ease. He was festive then, as if someone had thrown open a curtain and announced, "Here's Ricky!" He was always getting ready for his friends, thinking up things to say when he was with me.

They held the key. They took us down long, narrow piazzas to ornate rooms, and down plantation roads, and winding stairs, into magical realms that were as heavy with history as with humidity. In drawing rooms crowded with antiques and in musty old libraries where books rotted visibly, I met pale old men and white-haired ladies whose eyes flickered like candles burning blue in memory. They said they remembered Aunt Violet perfectly; some even had knowledge of the generation before, and I was anxious to know what they, in their backward glance, could see. I always wanted to stay longer, but Rutledge and Seabrook and Pinckney were nervous in these spheres and anxious to leave. They wanted to get back to their houses or apartments where they could gossip and drink and shriek.

"Good-bye, Granny!" they'd call out, signalling for us it was time to leave. Ricky would have to stop examining the prints on the wall, or peering into the inlay of the antiques. They expected different things from Ricky and he gladly obliged them.

At brunches, they gabbed on of underwear, Broadway musicals, and movies. I stood by silently, imagining it as I fancied older queens or carnival in Venice to be. For as if lifting elegant masks to their faces, they assumed grand personas through which to peer. They mimicked the old ladies, acted like harlots and mammies.

Ricky turned into Miss Dandridge then—and that is what everyone was called: Miss Linton or Miss Legare— they needed handles to touch them, as if they were hot or holy. They talked disdainfully of the men they knew who went to bars and "carried on" publicly and speculated on who could be trusted to come to one of their parties.

If I spoke, they listened for a while, but they always came back to what they had in common with others.

"Guess who I saw Lenny Semmes with the other night?" Rutledge would ask.

"Who?"

"Bal Thinken!"

"Oh, no!" they'd scream. "That hussy!"

I'd look over at Ricky and see him completely enraptured. I felt invisible, beyond hearing. They were locked in a time warp where they could be venal and petty and bitchy. Most of all what I felt for them was pity.

One evening when we sat on the porch having drinks, we looked down at two men in shorts walking down the street. They were probably tourists, for the two held hands and those on the porch were aghast.

Ricky finally said, "That's trashy."

The others agreed and ended up talking about boys they knew who were sick, who might be dying. They did not like to admit they knew anybody, for they felt it could not affect them, the scions of the city's best families. But they talked on, repeating rumors and half-truths until they horrified themselves, as with ghost stories. All insisted that they knew of a handsome man out there who was infecting people deliberately.

"No one would do that," I said. "That's silly."

They looked hurt; Ricky tried to silence me.

"What's his name?" I asked.

"Jinx," Van answered; and it stopped me.

"I knew someone named that once," I said. They were looking at me.

Van smiled, and I saw it all.

"Is Van short for Ivan?"

"Yes!" he said, nodding. I felt vulnerable, and the way he smiled gave me an uncomfortable feeling. I tried to keep my distance, realizing he knew all about me and the hut on the beach. I knew Ricky would protect me, so I went home with him.

But one night soon after, when I was alone, Van had parked behind the garden wall, waiting for me.

"Get in," he said, opening the car door.

"No thanks," I answered.

"Get in," he said sternly. His pants were undone. "Or I'll tell everybody."

He knew of a deserted parking lot at the edge of the battery.

It continued for a few weeks. I could not think. I was going back and forth between what had happened and what could happen to me. Then everything changed.

"The social season," Ricky announced exultantly one evening. "It's here. Everyone get ready!"

They had to stop the whispering; they had to maintain their positions as bachelors in Charleston society. So they periodically went out on dates with women to concerts or movies. Ricky explained that they needed a partner to get invited to balls and parties.

"But no need to overdo. Just places you can be seen," Ricky assured me. And since I was part of them now, I was expected to participate. So Ricky looked around for the appropriate person, and he fixed me up with Winkie, who was seven years older than me. Ricky told me that she had been jilted long ago and that there was a Thomas Elfe tea table that had been in her family for generations.

"I want to see it," he said. "So talk to her about furniture."

The trouble was I liked Winkie.

———

One night she and I decided to duck out of a party. We went out into the garden and were sneaking out to the street when the front door opened.

"Wait up," Ricky cried. With a drink in his hand and his date in tow, he and a few others followed us out.

"God, that was dull," he yawned. "Did you see that awful arrangement on the table? Plastic!"

Others laughed knowingly.

We walked out into the dark street, getting silent. The night was soothing, and the tall, narrow houses loomed up like tall ships at their moorings. It was just a block down to the battery.

It was late and gay boys were patrolling the oyster shell walks; I recognized some from the bar. I looked away, scared they would betray me, but they all looked down as we passed. Some were on benches, others wandered like lost souls under the lowering trees. Many crossed the street to get away from us and lit cigarettes by the seawall and peered into parked cars. I wanted to leave, especially when Ricky began.

"It's awful they come down here," he pointed. "They ruin it for everybody." Jan, his blond date, laughed nervously.

A sad-eyed boy slunk past us like someone trying to escape, and I felt guilty as a Jew condemning another in Nazi Germany. Winkie caught my eye. "Let's get out of here," she whispered. We walked back silently.

"I had a good time," she said when we approached her house. I took her up the stairs to her front door. In one of the upper windows there was a crack in the curtains through which I could see her mother peering. "I'd like to see you again, but I'll understand if you don't call me."

She turned around and shut the door swiftly.

———

We gathered later that night at Seabrook's parents' home—they were still away. I opened the window and pushed through the tall shutters to the piazza to think. The heat and closeness out there almost felt good compared to the chill, dead air of the air conditioning. Hazy circles surrounded the street lights and looked like the swirling stars of a Van Gogh painting. I leaned over the railing but pulled back. There was a man with no shirt on running noiselessly down the street. His beauty was so real it hurt. I felt like crying.

Sometimes, late at night on the battery, I could hear porpoises huffing and puffing on the other side of the seawall and I'd feel a thrill that some other life, so mysterious and strange, was so near. That feeling was the same one the runner gave me. He made me want to look up into the sky and count the stars, as numerous as blessings. I wanted to run after him and surrender at his feet.

I was watching him disappear down the street when Ricky put his hand on my back. He was drunk and lurching. He caught hold of my shoulder and whispered thickly, "Let's go home."

I was going to tell him it was too hot, but just then a light came on behind some shutters of the house next door and he put a finger to his lips. He leapt backward and slunk along the wall like someone on a ledge, squeezing back through the window and into the library.

I looked down at the street, thinking of the runner, and, as if waking up, I looked back through the window at Ricky. Van was looking at me.

"Where do you think you're going?" I asked the cat that had crept out of the room and was looking over the edge of the porch carefully. I rubbed his head and took him back into the library.

———

I couldn't go on after that; that runner had loosened something in me—a regret, a dream, a memory.

"Go on and tell them; I don't care," I told Van that night when he was waiting for me. "But I'll tell them about that parking lot by the battery."

I started spending more time on the beach, and there was a cooling, like fall itself, between Ricky and me. Yet summer still lingered, flaring up occasionally.

One late September evening, Ricky and I tarried through the empty stalls of the market, but I ran up eagerly when I saw Stevie and Dulcie standing on the curb.

Stevie was devouring a huge ice cream cone, attacking it from all sides with his tongue to keep it from melting. He hardly noticed me, but Dulcie looked relieved. She had been holding on to her purse with both hands and looking around her as if she were in one of the worst neighborhoods in New York.

"What time is it?" she asked hysterically.

She was stricken when I told her.

"I don't think that bus is coming," she told Stevie, who didn't respond. She licked a napkin and stuck it to his chin to clean up some ice cream.

Ricky stood aloof across the street in the market stalls, like an owner waiting for his pet to finish its duty. I wanted to introduce them. "Come on over," I said.

"No," he said crossly. "You come here." But I insisted.

"Charmed," he said grandly, reminding me of Momma and Francine and how I had once treated Stevie. It made me angry and I could tell his condescension hurt Dulcie. She looked at me in wonder.

"Excuse me, but are you coming in?" Ricky asked.

He wasn't expecting an answer; he was expecting me to follow. So he was surprised when I said, "No. I need to take them back to the beach. They're friends of mine."

"Friends?" He looked them up and down. "Well," he said, opening the door to the ice cream store, "I'm going in here." You'd have thought I had abandoned my senses the way he looked out the window at me.

That was the beginning of the end for Ricky and me. We still went out but our impasses came more frequently. Our silences stretched from minutes to days to a week. We stopped our Sunday ritual of taking each other out to eat. But one day he cornered me for lunch and demanded to know what was happening.

"Seabrook and Nowell have asked about you," he said, trying to make me feel guilty. "They may not ask you over anymore if you don't behave right."

"I don't care," I said.

He was shocked. "You're throwing away quite an opportunity."

When I told him I didn't like his friends, he escalated with heavy artillery. "Van said he knew you from before; he said you used to be pretty wild."

"So?"

He looked at me smugly. "Aren't you a little touchy?"

"Van's the one who's touchy, if you ask me."

Ricky was puzzled. I got up. "Sit down, please; people are watching."

"I have to go," I said. But I sat.

Ricky whispered, "Van says you knew that Jinx guy; that you two were pretty friendly. If you're contaminated . . ."

I broke in. "That was years ago—ancient history. Don't be so silly."

"If I get sick . . ." he started.

"You won't," I said, and got up to leave again.

Ricky got up, too, and started to come after me, but he looked around the restaurant. The last thing I heard was him crying out, "Laurens! Betsy! Where have you been

hiding yourselves? I've got the cutest little stool for you at
Her Majesty's!''

Whenever I saw him or Rutledge or Seabrook or any of
their friends in the bank or the Piggly Wiggly after that,
they looked away discreetly. And by the way other men I
did not know turned away, I knew Van had been telling
them terrible things about me.

But that was their way. I had to let Miss Dandridge
have her revenge on me.

Fall brought a chill to the air; but it was the news that set people shivering. There was more and more talk of the strange new disease; its mere mention distilled an unease. People got up and moved, changing the conversation even though they felt it had nothing to do with them. The nameless thing only got those glamorous boys in San Francisco and New York City. Yet men started recasting their histories. As AIDS was named, it was like being inside, in Charleston, listening to the first stirring of a storm in the trees.

I felt an aura of fear as I returned to the bar in the evenings. People eyed me with apprehension; since I was from "off," that hazy gray rest of the world outside the city, I was suspect. It was as if Ricky and Van had poisoned the whole well about me; or maybe it was just with the social season hitting high gear, there was less of a need for a stray like me. I walked alone at night through streets choked with leaves.

People came by in crowds, in twos and threes. I edged off the sidewalk to let them pass, trying not to catch their eyes, figuring they pitied me, all alone, as they came back from movies or dinner parties, laughing. But I let them; for as I walked the streets of the soft old city, I found something in hiding. I got glimmers of other orders existing in ghost layers around me—like pacing off old gardens and finding traces of a lost way in the weeds. It was like old books and diaries of displaced realities. Something like homesickness—not for a place but a feeling—was in the streets.

It was the wisdom of the past, the wisdom of evenings. Walking under the arching old oaks of the battery, listening to the river beyond, and looking at the chaste, mellow grandeur of the houses across the street, I drew on the great store of unhappiness that beauty or sorrow could bring out in me. Maybe it was not so important after all to be happy. Pitched against the cosmos, how could my unhappiness be a tragedy? I felt bittersweet, felt I was doing right when I left the city.

I'd open the door at Dulcie's with a grand gesture. They were so glad they were giddy. Stevie sat up late with me and watched TV.

One night when I went out there sleet was falling and the bridges iced over, so Dulcie made up the couch for me. The room was warm from the gas heater while thin needles of ice sliced the night. Stevie came in to peep at me.

"I know you're there," I said. "Come in."

I reached out and he crawled under my covers and fell asleep.

I'm back, I thought. *To where I should be.*

PART
4

THE SUMMER
IT REACHED

I CHANGED. IT HAPPENED SO quickly that it had to have been there all the while, just waiting to be revealed. It was like a relapse or reverting to how I used to be with Aunt Violet, Uncle Reynaldo, and Stevie. I spent more time at the beach and even volunteered at the Hope Center. I called people on the phone and tried to raise money. But I wanted others to remark on my change, to wonder and say things. But no one did. Not even Stevie.

When I picked him up from the Center after work, he'd be preoccupied, in a world of his own, perfectly happy. I had to pierce his obliviousness to have him need me. But he just took it all in stride, almost as if it were owed him.

I got a better result from Dulcie. Night after night after Stevie was asleep, I sat up with her, encouraging her with Leroy. I listened as she read his letters to me.

"Leroy *is* after you," I told her one night.

She looked at me wet-eyed, as if I had given her everything. After that, we were joined in a web of intrigue. She ascribed vast wisdom to me. I acted slow and wise and weary, happy that love was coming for her, if not for me. Dulcie never spoke of my love-life, but she brought up the topic of Leroy constantly, asking for reassurance like a begging puppy.

"You go visit him," I told her. "I'll stay with Stevie."

She was so excited after that Stevie could not help but notice her gaiety and respond to it. We flew through those winter weeks as if on a bright carousel gaining speed.

I stayed many a night on the beach. I woke up before dawn to get back to the city in time for work.

I ran into Talbert on his way out the gate one morning, and he wanted to know where I had been.

"Oh, just to see some friends on the beach."

"That must be *some* friend," he said and winked.

I winked back, letting him think I had found somebody. I knew he would not be able to understand what I was feeling. I had recaptured that first summer on the beach when Aunt Violet and Uncle Reynaldo had been so proud of me.

I took Dulcie and Stevie out on her birthday. She had been opposed to it, but I asked her in front of Stevie. She had to give in, seeing his excitement, knowing what her refusal would bring.

She held her coat tightly about her, and when we went into the restaurant on Market Street, she looked at the waiters suspiciously. People turned around to gawk, but Stevie did not mind. When the waiter handed him his menu, he just gyrated in his seat, marvelling at the brick walls, the white linen tablecloths, and the brass chandeliers.

Across the restaurant from us I saw them: Ricky and

Van eating. They were in a booth and Ricky looked up coolly—Van's eyes danced like the candles, with a mischievous light of their own casting. He looked us over: fat old Stevie, Dulcie with her green coat adorned with a huge rhinestone cat pin, and me. Then he whispered to Ricky and I heard laughter. I grabbed Stevie's hand and whispered in his ear.

On the count of three, we made hideous faces at them and people by their table broke out laughing. Van and Ricky immediately shifted their attention down to their plates, casting glances around the restaurant.

They left soon after, but we stayed on for cake and ice cream and coffee. It was more than righting wrongs. I was having fun with Stevie.

As the news of AIDS spread and hints of spring appeared, I focused entirely on Stevie. Dulcie was amazed. She could hardly believe I kept returning until one day she simply asked me, "Why?" And I didn't know what to say except that I loved Stevie and that was enough. She nodded as if she understood perfectly. I stayed in town to work; my life was on the beach.

But sometimes I was weak. Sundays were the worst. As I left Sullivan's Island, a loneliness, like a chill, would come over me. Charleston's dark silhouette, jagged like shark's teeth, looked brave and sumptuous in the golden light that poured from the dark, clouded evening. Against the purple it could have been the last ray of hope, civilization's dying gleam.

As soon as I got home I'd phone them to ask if they needed anything. I had to seize on something—a book, a chore, an idea, anything—to break the bleak mood that was coming on: Sunday night alone with no one to comfort me.

I tried not to give in, but visions came up like bubbles underwater, bearing all the faces I had known, all the bodies. I had to get release. When it was over, I lay there, sad and betrayed, my hand draped over my chest, damp and limp as a lily.

Anytime Stevie had to go somewhere, I volunteered. I also took him out to eat and bought him things. Once when he had a dentist's appointment, I begged Dulcie to let me take him. I could get off from work more easily, so she agreed. I sat with him, proud that he held my hand and whimpered for me when the dentist began drilling.

"There, there," I soothed him. "It will be over soon, Stevie. We're going to wean you off sweets so you won't get any more cavities. We're going to save your teeth."

His face was still swollen as we went for groceries. I put my finger on his chin and pulled his forehead to mine so we eyed each other squarely.

"Now, you be good, Stevie."

He nodded. Once in the door, though, he waddled away.

"None of your tricks, Stevie." He went off like a sleuth with his hands behind his back. I sent him for apples and bread and other innocuous things—to keep his mind and hands off the candy and cookies he was used to getting. But a stock clerk caught him with an open bag of M&Ms spilling on the floor while he gorged on them. Amazed kids watched and mothers stood by aghast as if he were Jupiter devouring his children.

"Sir! Sir!" the clerk was crying when I turned down the aisle and saw what was happening. You'd have thought it was a murder.

"Quit staring," I snapped. I was more angry with the people than with Stevie. "Go home! Watch TV!" I shouted. I could not stand it as they watched us.

We went to another store. I tried not to be angry, but a bag of chocolate chip cookies surfaced at the checkout. Stevie looked down quickly as I took it from the checker.

"This isn't mine," I told her. "Take it off, please."

Someone behind us in line groaned.

The girl flicked up the top of her machine to check the tape. It snagged and started beeping. She called out to the woman at the next register.

As they put their heads together, people in the two lines started sighing and groaning. One little boy staring at Stevie asked his mother if he was E.T. She yanked his arm so hard he started to cry. All eyes were on us.

"Stevie," I said, but he turned away before I could catch his eye. He crossed his arms and hugged himself tightly, holding his breath, squeezing his eyes shut, and showing his gums as he refused to answer.

"You're going to pop," I warned, but he held out, as if it were his individuality he was afraid of surrendering.

I politely held out the bag of cookies. "Stevie, will you put these back?"

He shook his head and stamped his feet.

I saw the manager coming. I changed my voice. "Remember the dentist?" I asked. He froze in fear and peeked at me. "You'll have to go back there unless you return these."

I saw him remembering, biting his lip, grimacing. But he still did not give in. I was desperate with all the people watching.

"Atlantis," I said suddenly. "Do you remember, Stevie?"

He looked puzzled. It tensed up his face as if he were about to sneeze.

"That wonderful place underwater, Stevie? You can't go there if you've been bad." He looked deflated. "Attaboy." He took the cookies back.

When we got back to the island, we unpacked the groceries and hand in hand, we walked the shore and Stevie stared out to sea.

————

The last few weeks of winter were peaceful. We walked the shore with our thick sweaters on, examining things that had washed up. The people we passed no longer looked at us. We were known on the beach and where we got our groceries.

It got warmer, and Stevie and I spent more time together. It got greener, too. We roved the island and came upon the gates of the old cemetery.

I stared in, not knowing whether Stevie remembered or not. But I did. Stevie made a move to go in, but I pulled him back by the hand. He looked at me quizzically as a dog on a leash.

"Come away, Stevie."

I pulled him back down the lane while he looked back regretfully. I did, too; for what I had done down there in the quarantine hut still bothered me, especially as it began to get warmer. Sap rose up like memory, but I was not worried.

SPRING CAME IN QUICKLY
those next few weeks, and we were ready. We had felt its
warm breath blowing over the roofs as early as February
and seen its fuzzy green vines uncurling like a finger beckoning. We advanced into the warmth of March; everything
happened effortlessly.

The bus came to get Stevie in the morning; later on,
I went to work and so did Dulcie. Afterwards, we'd pick
him up. I liked the blandness, the repetition, the serenity.
As if it were going to last forever, as if it had gone on for
years, we settled into it comfortably. I suppose I took it
for granted, not realizing I had already reached the apogee.
Stasis came, but as it does in disease: if it was fruition and
completeness, it was for a moment only.

Once April came, I started spending more time in the
city. As afternoons stretched toward evening, I'd find Talbert and Jerry and their friends talking in the courtyard,

and sometimes I'd stay for a drink. When they'd be heading out to the gym, they'd ask me, "Do you want to come along?" "No," I'd answer laughing. "You go on without me." I'd stay on to catch a few moments of peace.

"You'd better come," they warned. "Get your bathing suit out. Summer's coming." They'd point to the sky and the budding green trees as if they were seeing a beast, or a fin on the sea.

But I was not concerned, still sure summer no longer was a worry.

When it got warm enough, Stevie and I went to the beach. The first few weeks I felt high on a tide of heat and light, as if I were exuding the heat and summer was burning off me. Hand-in-hand we walked back, ravenous and happy.

But afternoons lasted longer; the heat increased. In the city, green flooded the streets, eddying over curbs, and splitting the concrete as if there were a molten green core beneath. On the island, the trees grew fuller, cutting off the light. Summer brought a darkening. Stevie and I roved the island and we again came upon the gates of the old cemetery.

I stopped, confused. Many of the trees had been cut and there were stakes with orange strips flapping the breeze. Yellow bulldozers were everywhere. Houses were framed right to the edge of the derelict buildings. We saw kids playing in there and they looked at us alarmed.

"Come on, Stevie."

I think summer began then, with the crickets shrieking. My vision swam and temples beat as we walked away. After that, hot days repeated and we passed deeper into the green eternity. And because Stevie and Dulcie didn't have it, there was no relief to be had in air conditioning.

They also put up a traffic light that summer. All afternoon long it went from red to green as we went from the house to the beach; I heard the whining of its machinery and it got into my head. The beat summed up everything—day and night, city and beach, light and heat. It was just the same way the insects shrieked, careening between love and death, their rasps revealing them to mates and enemies alike.

Dulcie and I sat listening to their operatic shrills one evening, fanning ourselves as our rockers coursed the porch. Stevie sat between us, feet dangling as if on a boat in a sea of summer. He was listless and shiny. He wanted to go back down to the water.

"It's too soon after eating," Dulcie said. "And besides, you spend too much time in the water, Stevie."

There was no denying that, but I knew what Dulcie really wanted was to hold on to me, to have me stay with her instead of taking Stevie swimming. It usually flattered me, but I was too hot to be bothered. I knew the time for her visit to Leroy was coming.

"He hasn't written in a while," she worried.

"Maybe he's busy, Dulcie."

"Doing what?"

"Getting ready for your visit."

She looked at my face. Not comforted but unwilling to go in, she twisted the towel in her hand. Stevie turned around and asked, "What are y'all saying?"

"Nothing," Dulcie answered and went back inside. He looked out over the yard. "Sure do wish I could go to the beach."

"All right," I agreed. "Get ready."

When I came back, Stevie was already standing at the edge of the yard, watching the little black Grimshawe children who lived next door. Like a dog on a tether dying to get free, he looked back to Dulcie for permission, but she shook her head. "No, Stevie," she cautioned as the kids came over and stood solemnly by the fence, looking like

starving African children, wide eyes and big bellies. They
lived with their crone of a grandmother who curtsied when
any white people were near.

"You stay away from them," Dulcie warned. "And
don't you let them play with him when I'm gone," Dulcie
told me.

"Where you going?" Stevie asked, whirling around.
She colored and glared at me, as if it were my fault.

"Nowhere, and never you mind."

He had an anxious look in his eyes.

"Go on," she shooed.

We went to the shore as usual, but we came back
early. Stevie ran toward the house, crying her name,
worried.

One afternoon soon after, she finally told him she was
going visiting.

"No you're not," he said. He shook his head and held
himself the way he had when we fought over the groceries.

"I'll be back soon," she told him, chucking his chin.
He pulled away. "I'm going to Leroy. You remember him."

He shook his whole body violently and stamped his
feet. He put his hands to his ears. "No," he said.

"But, Stevie!" she said. "You like Leroy."

"No, I don't," he cried. "He's mean!"

"He isn't."

"He is!" He was almost crying.

Dulcie tried to speak. But Stevie paraded around like
a bad boy, not listening. He stuck out his tongue and
shouted, "I hate Leroy."

"That's ugly," she said. "Don't do that!" she shouted
when he persisted. "Stevie!" It was the first time I had
seen Dulcie mad. I watched amazed as she reached out to
slap Stevie. It wasn't hard—just startling. But he ran over
to me and faked tears. She reached out to him, but he
darted away. "Don't," he cried and clung to me. He was

silent and watched her begrudgingly, as if he suspected her of cheating. At a loss, she went into her room.

"Come help me, Stevie," she coaxed. "Help me pack, sweetie." She started laying out everything she would need, counting skirts and blouses and shoes. "Monday, Tuesday, Wednesday. . . ." After a while she forgot about Stevie. Maybe it was the light through the blinds, but suddenly as she smiled, she seemed lit in the aura of her leaving. Stevie hung his head and continued to cling to me. I pulled him down the steps; he looked back at Dulcie.

"Come on," I urged.

I was in a hurry, for I had already met Jim by then. He was already a part of me, but even then, when I tried to remember, I couldn't recall when we had met exactly. It must have been before it got too hot; for by then, when in desperation we'd reach for speed, he was already a part of my thoughts. I'd think of him as Stevie and Dulcie and I climbed into the car at night. We headed for the causeway and to the bridge to the city. We raced along to be buffeted by the breeze and to try for a moment in a whirl of wind to break free of summer and heat. Stevie would cry delightedly as we raced up the bridge; and I'd think of Jim as we rolled down into the city.

Maybe he was part of that summer from the beginning. He always rose up in a swirl of association and a cluster of images that made me dizzy. Maybe I had seen him in town. Maybe I had seen him running. Thinking of him made me shivery.

Before we met, I had felt vulnerable crossing the beach with Stevie. With men lying out nearly naked tanning, I kept my eyes down, feeling I was crossing a mine field. I was afraid that the old smile I had used for Glynn and his friends would betray me. But for Jim, the smile I gave was genuine.

When we first spoke, the afternoon was nearly over;

heat trailed across the sky in a white smear. Stevie was in the water. I sat out, having forgotten anything to read. I patted a dog that ran up and licked my hand. The heat had peaked and I was ready to coast into evening.

In the distance I saw a runner or two; I saw someone swimming near Stevie and watched him idly. He seemed familiar to me. Each stroke of his arm made a wave that caught the light and flashed the water mesmerizingly until he dived and disappeared.

He came up closer to the shore, between the dark sky and the sea, smiling at me. With his hands on his head, he flattened out his wet, dark hair like a helmet. Each step revealed more and more of him.

I watched secretly, pretending not to see the water dripping from his waist, running down his muscular thighs, rivulets down his streamlined body. Naked had he gone in swimming. That narrow band of untanned flesh shocked me. I looked at his dark dense hair and felt giddy.

He stopped at a pile of clothes and bent over; his buttocks flashed white as his shoulders spanned and he stepped into his shorts and worked into shoes. He saw me. I was ready to glance down defeated, but he smiled. At me. I looked again—he was still grinning.

He stood straight up, dressed now and looking more tanned in his running clothes. He snapped the elastic of his shorts and flashed teeth impishly as a boy, as if to say, yes, he knew his splendidness. And wasn't it amazing? His good spirits made me happy.

A flare of hope leapt up, and I could barely breathe, much less think, as he bent down again to gather up the towel, a wallet, and keys. He started up the beach toward me. I looked down as the ground shook. Water droplets fell.

"Hey," he said. His voice was like a breath on the back of my neck, electrifying me. I froze, unable to speak until he had passed me.

"Hi," I said suddenly.

He turned. His long, wet hair was swinging and his fine, sharp features were etched against the sky, his mouth open, teeth gleaming. His blue eyes riveted me. He looked as perfect as something from a magazine, and maybe that was why I was flooded with the feeling of recognition, as if I already knew him. He looked at me questioningly, temptingly. But I did nothing.

"My name's Jim," he said.

I told him mine, but it was like he already knew it. A minute later he left, and Stevie came up and threw his inner tube down. He hurled himself in it. I tried to concentrate on what Stevie was saying, but I couldn't. I was telling myself, *He means nothing to me.*

"Where did this come from?" Stevie asked, holding out a brown beer bottle.

"The water?" I asked faintly, but he shook his head and showed it to me again. "A ship?"

"No," Stevie whined, his forehead furrowed. "You know . . ." trying to prompt me.

"Atlantis?"

"Yes!" He rolled the word under his tongue as if it tasted sweet. "Tell me about it," he prodded. As I spoke, I looked down the beach in search of Jim, but he was gone.

"Would you like to go there?" I asked.

"Yes," Stevie cried. "Take me!"

I promised I would as we headed back to Dulcie.

I DID NOT THINK OF JIM again until I saw him a few days later. He was with Stevie when I got past the dunes.

He had already been in swimming. Stevie had a bleach bottle in his hand, and the two of them were bent over it. "No," he was saying to Stevie. "Don't say anything." Then, when I came up, Jim stuck out his hand.

"I see you met Stevie," I said.

"Old friends," he told me. I tried to talk nonchalantly, but Stevie ran back to the water, and Jim put the bottle down and stared at me. He did not say a thing; he just smiled and preened, waiting for me to provide the incentive for him to speak. I couldn't.

"Stevie's nice," Jim said finally. His open, frank face, his honest eyes, were so friendly. I gulped and nodded. "Do you live here?" he asked, sighting the dunes. I nodded. "So do I." Nothing.

"Well, see you later," he said, tapping me on the shoulder. I turned around to watch him, and he turned back and winked.

There were some more episodes after that, I think. When he was close, we'd speak. "Nice day," he'd say and I'd think he was saying something secret to me. I caught myself every now and then and told myself, "He's a flirt; it doesn't mean anything." But that did not keep me from stealing peeks whenever I saw him on the beach.

I hung back and would not go near when he was with someone else; I tried to show him how it hurt, how he was betraying me. Other boys would wait around and go into the water when he was in swimming or they'd be standing at his clothes when he emerged. Often they went home together, but even then, I thought (or maybe imagined) Jim was looking back at me.

Or maybe it was at Stevie. For whenever he saw us together he spoke to us both, and once he gave Stevie a sand dollar he had dug up while swimming.

"You're quite a pair," he said to me once, almost accusingly.

I shrugged. "He needs someone to watch him."

"Can't he swim?"

"Not really; and besides, people don't like him. Look." A woman was waving her kids away from Stevie as he waddled their way in the water.

"Come here," I hollered. "This way, Stevie."

Jim looked from the woman to me and shook his head thoughtfully, as if he had learned something.

I went home that day, went to work and to sleep, but that was not what was happening to me. No, not hardly. For I had entered a new level—had gone out of the heat to somewhere it could not reach me. Jim got into my consciousness and was like a scent. I thought of him long after I left the beach. Often I was too keyed up to sleep, but when I dozed off an eroticism charged my dreams like lightning.

Restless, I'd hear a voice call, see a hand reach, and I'd feel as I did as a kid when the boys on the beach summoned me. Wings of light beat and I found it hard to breathe. The air was dense and smothering.

During the day, the sky was purblind, white and milky. In the afternoon, I'd take Stevie to the beach. Often I'd see Jim running, his muscles straining against his clothes as if against the constraints of physics. I wanted to surrender, for his existence had more importance than mine. His strength made me weak. I felt I was fueling his beauty. He ran and the thud of his feet on the sand was the rhythm of my heartbeat.

When he passed, I felt a part of myself going on with him. I wanted to run after and say, "Take me."

One day he shocked me.

I heard him lie to a young man who had almost knocked me over hurrying up to where Jim was sunning. They spoke a bit. I drifted closer, trying to hear.

They got up and the boy went into the water to rinse his sandals off.

"What's your name?" the boy asked when he came out. Down the beach a mother was screaming at her son, "William, come here."

"Will," he said as he gathered up his towel; he saw me watching and winked. They went off the beach and Jim shrugged as if to say, Can I help it that everyone finds me good-looking?

I was still standing on the beach when he came back to retrieve the watch that had fallen from his shoe. He came over and was going to speak. "Will," the boy, standing on the dunes, screamed. He was watching us.

"Someday," Jim said. "Someday I'll—" But the boy yelled, "Are you coming?"

Jim laughed and said, "Now, you go take care of Stevie."

I ran into the water. I did not know what to think; was he dismissing or admiring me? Maybe I was a challenge—maybe he had never known anyone who was as good to anyone as I was to Stevie. A million wonderful thoughts came to me. So I gave in to them. Maybe I was getting my reward, my due. Finally.

The shallows held the heat, so Stevie and I went out deep to where we could not touch bottom and the currents made us shiver.

"Oooh!" Stevie made a face. I laughed, and he hugged me.

But the next day, Jim seemed angry. When he knew I was looking, he got up and stretched and flexed his muscles. He left without speaking. The day after, he went to where some boys lay out. He sat with them and laughed and looked back my way to gauge the effect it had, as if he were tempting me.

I stayed where I was and watched Stevie.

Everything else happened in a dim field; nothing else was real.

We had a party for Dulcie's departure, but I left the cake too long in my car and the icing melted, so we had ice cream only. On the way down to the station, she laughed out loud and then put her hand over her mouth and caught herself. Embarrassed, she put her hand in her lap and looked guilty. Stevie would not look at her at all.

By the time we got downtown, she was jittery. As the bus left, she held out her hand to Stevie and looked out the bus window with something like panic, as if she were drowning. She opened her mouth, but the bus pulled around the corner. Stevie ran after her and then came back slowly to the car. He was crying. He sat with his face on his fists, looking through the windshield.

July had gone by then, and August had pulled us down in a deeper, more hellish ring of heat. That afternoon had burned low like a candle; we could see its wavelengths wavering as we drove back. On the way to the beach we passed people hopping up and down as crazily as three-legged dogs as they crossed the molten streets.

"It's just you and me, Stevie," I said.

Scared, he looked at me.

But we soon settled down into a routine. We went to the beach every day—him in the water, me on the shore. We took up the same positions every day as if we were rehearsing, trying to get something right so, when summer ended, we could pass through to fall and be free.

The Saturday after Dulcie left, Stevie and I went down early to the beach. Everyone had fled the city.

I saw Ricky Dandridge wending his way towards us, wrapped in a white caftan, and all his friends came after him like bearers in a retinue—they carried umbrellas and wicker baskets and drinks. He pointed and they unloaded and unfolded, looking like cranes, awkward and graceful simultaneously. They patted down their towels and looked around to see who they had acquired for company, nodding at some deserving folk, noting but ignoring me.

Then he and Van and the rest of them lay flat like sacrifices surrendering, rendering themselves up to the sun. Most everyone on the beach was sprawled out that way, asleep. When I woke, I saw Jim. He had been running. The white towel around his neck was stark against his dark body, and the cleft of his breast was shadowed deeply. He sat for a while and propped himself up on his elbows, staring at the sun, refusing to surrender. Instead he worked his face into a tight, hard smile like he was concentrating on sending the sun down and that's why he was sweating.

He surged up when he saw me.

"Hey." He leaned over and in his mirrored lenses I could see myself looking up begging. For a second I felt I was in a drugstore, looking up at round mirrors that deformed me.

He laughed and traced my lips with his finger, sending shivers through me. A man in a skimpy bathing suit sat up and took notice. Then Ricky rose off his towel like a man from his tomb, his face swathed in creams.

They were aghast. He and his friends rubbed shoulders, nudged each other awake and whispered among themselves. All of them looked at me as if they were seeing something horrific.

I felt I had passed beyond them then, into another sphere, and their witnessing was notarial with its seal.

I took Jim's suntan lotion and rubbed it into his shoulders as they continued watching.

FOR EVERYONE ELSE, THE days came on as maddeningly and identically as drum beats. There was no rain, and the ground ached for relief. But I passed through the white glare unfazed—when I walked on the beach, people parted, as if awed by my destiny. I went on, as if being called, as if a finger were beckoning me.

I woke from my nap one afternoon, dazed with a dream that lay on me heavily. The air had deadened. As if I lay in an open grave, Stevie looked down at me.

"What is it?" I asked. "What's happening?"

Stevie rubbed his head and looked around as if someone were in the room with us.

I sat up, and the room careened. The light was wrong and there was a ringing in my ears. Then I realized.

"It's only the siren, Stevie." I looked at the clock, but it was after three. "Come on." We linked fingers. "Let's go see." There were no shadows outside, but the glare made me blink.

We followed people down to the coast guard station, where they were staring at the siren on the flagpole as if there were an actual bugler there. They were raising flags. "Storm warnings," I told Stevie.

I knew I wasn't supposed to be excited, but I was. For storms were the lore of the place, rites of passage old-timers talked about, the way Aunt Violet and Uncle Reynaldo talked about *used-to-be*. They were like ghost stories: you felt special and a part of it, listening. Storms with simple names like Hope and Grace came from the sea, and they changed you like Love did, or Hope, or Charity. Here was an opportunity for something new, for the air to clear.

I stayed in with Stevie that night, calming his nerves, and the next morning, I got up early; but the shelves in the stores, even on the mainland, were already nearly empty. There was no bread, bottled water, or batteries—people were getting ready. On the way to the beach, we saw men nailing plywood over plate glass and taping window panes with crosses as if expecting a beast to rise from the sea.

It rained sporadically. Breezes tossed the trees. Gulls rode currents of air and palmetto fronds beat languidly. Not only people left; it seemed oxygen was dwindling, as if maybe summer had breathed out and we were waiting for it to inhale, to bring fall back and vitality.

The storm hovered offshore for three days, a lens to our listlessness, magnifying heat and anxiety. We milled about, waiting with our mouths half open the way Stevie waited to go swimming. We talked twice a day to Dulcie. Stevie liked it that she was worried. For her he acted bravely. I looked for Jim, but found out later he was taking care of his folks' house in the city.

One morning, the skies cleared—the storm shifted north to Hatteras, and we were marooned back in the heat.

A few days later, Stevie developed prickly heat, and the powder I shook on him stuck to his moist skin like powdered sugar on a doughnut. By afternoon the air under the tin roof throbbed so that I could not think. The night it cleared I took Stevie back into town with me just so we could sleep in air conditioning, but he missed the beach. He went into Dulcie's room every afternoon and fingered her things. Wondering about what she would bring him was one way of coaxing a smile out of Stevie. He'd sit with his chin down on his chest in his swimsuit, waiting for the phone to ring. When it did, he ran to it happily. He cradled the receiver delicately as he spoke to his sister. We crossed the days off until her homecoming. It was down to three when she called early in the evening.

"Stevie! It's Dulcie."

He came in and took it. A smile appeared but then failed. He looked blank for a second, and then he dropped the receiver as if it were a spider. He ran out. I picked up the phone; Dulcie was still talking.

". . . Down soon and then, maybe . . . I don't know. We'll have to decide, but no matter what happens—"

I interrupted: "Dulcie, it's me."

"You were right," she said. "He—Leroy—asked . . ."

"Asked what?"

"We're going to be married."

"I'm so happy for you," I said as Stevie crept back in to listen. He looked at me as if I were betraying him.

After that, he watched and followed me everywhere, even in the bathroom, as if he were afraid I was going to leave. I had to push him out of the room, hollering, "Stevie, please."

"She doesn't love you any less than before," I told him, but change scared him terribly.

"Will you take care of me?" he wanted to know.

"I promise, Stevie."

At night he crept into my bed and clung to me. I

woke up and fought him off, barely able to breathe—he was so huge and heavy and stuck to me.

When we went to the beach that last afternoon, the tide was out. Summer seemed to have drained away after it.

I remember a nervousness, like heat lightning, like static electricity—the feeling of chalk on a blackboard or long fingernails on stockings. I went into the water with Stevie. When I came out, I sat down on the towel. I saw Jim coming. He came nearer but I held my eyes down. He stopped when he saw me peek.

He came up and I looked him in the eye. He looked at me oddly, as if he saw what I was seeing.

"Sure is hot," he said.

"Yes."

"What are you doing tonight?" he asked.

"Nothing. Why?" He was just about to answer when I heard a shout. Stevie was coming out of the water, carrying his inner tube.

"Something bit me," he said. "Look!" He came up limping and holding his side. "Here." There was a red indentation.

"Oh, Stevie. It's just where your tube's valve rubbed you." He whined and looked back at the water, refusing to be persuaded. He kept bumping against me defiantly. I tried to reason with him, to get him to stop, but he started crying. Jim made a face and moved off. "Well, I gotta be going," he said.

"See you later?" I asked.

"Sure," he said. "Maybe."

I was angry with Stevie and pulled him along after me.

After supper it started drizzling, so we couldn't go swimming. But it stopped later. In the distance we heard thunder and saw a little lightning. Stevie was anxious and finally fell asleep at about ten-thirty; the fan was on high and it drowned out sound and set the floor vibrating. I sat on the porch in the stultifying calm. I told myself I was just going for a walk, that I would be back shortly.

As I walked, the wind started. I walked faster and looked into the bushes. Shadows seemed to be following me.

I walked down the street to the new construction site and stopped. The bulldozers had destroyed the vegetation. Only one gate was standing, the other one lay on the ground as if something had burst through it. Holes where the dead had been pitted the old cemetery. Nothing was left—not the stones, or even their memories.

I turned back when I heard faint thunder, but then I thought with the fan on, it would not disturb Stevie. I got closer and closer to the shore, but then the lightning got brighter. I moved over to the shoulder when a car turned the corner, blinding me in its headlights. As it came up, I could see the windshield wipers working. And behind them a face. Jim looked out, smiling.

"Well, look who's here." He leaned out the window and I started to tremble. "Want a lift?"

I nodded, trying not to get my hopes up too quickly. I was so happy I felt like crying but coolly slid into the passenger's seat. "I'm staying at—"

But he turned into his driveway on Middle Street. "*I* live right here," he said.

The lightning flashed and the island shook. I thought of Stevie, but could not let go of the moment or of Jim's hand. He was holding me.

We were still in the car, and before I could understand what was happening, his other hand was out and I, too, was reaching. We were kissing violently. Both of us pulled away, shocked at the intensity.

"Whoa," Jim said. He wiped his mouth, and looked at me, really looked seriously into my eyes. "You want it badly." I nodded, sheepishly. He started backing the car out the driveway.

"Where are we going?" I asked. He reached over and put my hand on his lap. "My folks' house is more comfortable," he said, and drove me into the city.

I DON'T KNOW WHAT IT WAS, the dream itself, or what we had done—maybe it was the relaxation he brought me. But I thought the storm had stayed out at sea. Locked up in the vastness of his parents' house, still shuttered and taped from the warnings, we heard nothing. The first I heard of the waterspout was when I went back to the island in a taxi.

"Some things is fine," the driver was saying. "Others is all messed up."

We raced over the causeway, passing the police who were pulling a dinghy from the road. I panicked, thinking of Stevie.

I'll never forget what I saw that morning. I saw a drowned world—some houses were sunken in big puddles, fish were stranded in trees. It was as if the island had become part of the sea, and now the two were loathe to separate. The tide washed back slowly as if looking back longingly, Orpheus and Eurydice.

It was difficult getting to the back of the island so I had the taxi leave. There were a few downed trees, but what stunned me most as I ran were the hundreds of butterflies fluttering yellow-green, intact despite their fragility. I made my way past cars and houses spattered with leaves, running up the stairs relieved that the house looked fine, calling out, "Stevie, I'm here."

At first I did not notice. Everything inside looked fine besides some puddles under the windows. I sat on my bed, relieved. Then I noticed Stevie's bed was empty.

I ran around, calling. I looked for him. In the closet, I found his pillow and tore through the clothes to see if he could be hiding. He must have burrowed in there. Thunder terrified him. I imagined him wincing at the lightning.

The little black Grimshawe children from next door were out in the yard picking up things that had blown about when I ran out on the porch. When I saw Stevie's inner tube was gone, I didn't know whether to be frightened or relieved.

"Have you seen Stevie?" I asked the children. They stopped what they were doing as if caught stealing. The old crone came into the yard to protect them. "Have *you* seen Stevie?" I asked.

"Yes, sir," she said. "Early this morning. Real early. Takin' off down the street like the devil was after him," she laughed. "I call to him. 'Mr. Stevie,' I say. 'Is you OK?' But he don't pay no mind to me. That sister of his told him not to. Ain't you been here?" she asked slyly. But by then I was already running.

I called the island police. Teams searched the water, people combed the beach. It seemed everyone was out, curiosity seekers came in droves from the city. The television news called him the only fatality, but the police just listed him as missing. The crews interviewed me.

"I think he was going to Atlantis," I told Dulcie when she returned.

When Leroy came the next week by bus, they still had not found Stevie.

"It's my fault," I said, not telling her where I had been. "I shouldn't have let him go out in the morning." I wanted her to disagree, but she did not say a thing. She shrugged and walked up the shore and stood a distance away from me. She stood with Leroy—he put his arms around her and both of them looked at me.

How could one night have done this? One night! I'd think I pictured him sailing to Atlantis, not struggling as the water reached. I wept for him and for me.

Leroy stayed in the house while Dulcie and I walked the shore. I came in one day and saw him looking through Dulcie's drawers. He closed it and winked. I did not do anything. I was trying not to think.

By the coming of the cool week, the case was closed, and people started to leave. Leroy went back, but Dulcie stayed. We sat together in the evenings, jumping when the phone rang. Dulcie would take it into the next room and, with her hand over the mouthpiece, say things I could not hear. In September, Dulcie closed the windows, locked the door, and left for Tennessee.

Maybe I should have left, too, but I couldn't. I was held by memory and fear. If I thought about Stevie, I could keep thoughts of Jim away. I was scared every time the phone rang it was Jim calling to laugh at or taunt me.

I thought about it all—all the faces, and Stevie—and everything that had happened to me.

And then as summer returned in blazing heat, I thought about the Carolina Paroquet.

AUDUBON DREW IT; SO DID Bartram and Catesby. I read the accounts of travellers who took them as pets, and of the others who shot them mercilessly. But the saddest thing of all, I thought, was what Reynaldo had told me: how when a bird died, his or her mate came down from the trees and mourned near the body, rendering it vulnerable to its enemies. Visitors had said that when a single one died, hundreds swarmed down from the trees. They were friendly, and flew up to people readily.

It made me think. Was it the paroquet's love or grief? Or was it our greed that made it extinct? I kept walking and thinking. And now I wonder what happened to me.

These afternoons under the trees, I sit, remembering. Summer rises up in a reprise; and I see it all coming again, like light years. In September heat, the glow of afternoons, and the light of history, it is still happening. I can get it back and see Stevie rise up from the gully; we become friends and I leave. I come back and then leave him that last night, asleep. Then I try not to remember what happened to me.

When I woke after the storm, I rolled over and kissed Jim and said, "Good morning."

And he smiled and kissed me. We loved each other again and I knew I had made it. I was happy. But playing my fingers over his chest, I felt something. I looked. It was a purplish, bruised swelling.

"What is it?" I asked.

"Nothing."

But I was getting nervous. "I never noticed it before," I said.

"It just appeared."

He went back to sleep. I shook him. "I need to get back to the beach."

He seemed still asleep, but before I left, he handed me something. I smiled at the little piece of paper he gave me. JIM it read, with his phone number.

"Yeah," he said, hoisting himself up on his elbow, "but all my friends call me Jinx." I started and he laughed. "I've always been unlucky." He picked at his sore. The siren was ringing as the taxi neared the beach.

Every time I remember it, it is the same, never diluted: there is the cold chill, the nausea, the horror and fear; the thinking *This cannot be*. I see Ricky and his friends in the library, telling tales about Jinx. On the beach, Van is looking horrified at us. *It cannot be*.

I denied it for weeks. I walked. I looked in the mirror, at my hands, at my face, in disbelief. I felt like arguing. It had just been one night, I reasoned, one momentary lapse.

It couldn't be. For what good was wisdom or life or learning if you could never change or get free of your past, or outgrow your history? No, I calmed myself. It would not happen to me.

But I was in Charleston. Fall came, Dulcie was gone, and as I walked the beautiful old streets, I saw I was in Pharaoh's city. I was in Jacob's dream: the past devouring the present, the fat kine being swallowed by the lean.

Slowly, the signs appeared.

As I got sick, I saw faces fly by and I woke up drenched in sweat and stuck to the sheets like something washed up on the beach. Night sweats were the first symptoms, though I tried to tell myself it was just the heat. Pneumonia made me feel like I was drowning. I was hospitalized for weeks.

I got better, though Charleston has no use for people like me. They treat us like we don't exist, as if we are beyond help, dead already. But we recognize each other as symbols of the city. We steal down the streets and sit by each other's beds; we tell each other stories. In a world apart, we are like ghosts or creatures undersea, a different species.

We sit out of time like the paroquet. As I sit here, day grays into evening. No one visits and no one hears. No one listens, even though we speak.

> *This is what happened to one.*
> *(There were so many of us once.)*
> *This is what happened to me.*

It makes me want to speak, but I listen. And I wonder if it is their regrets the dead remember or is it their dreams they muse on eternally? It is the latter I think, for as the heat reaches up and I fall asleep, everything else falls away. I feel buoyant and floating; I want to cry out with the panorama of happiness I see opening in front of me. It is just like it was when I came through the woods that night and approached the hut where the boys were waiting. Like the evening I first crossed the dunes and saw the ocean open and warm lying in front of me.

ᴾ **PLUME** (0452)

THE CONTEMPORARY SCENE

PLUME

COMING OF AGE

☐ **THE SALT POINT by Paul Russell.** This compelling novel captures the restless heart of an ephemeral generation that has abandoned the future and all of its diminished promises. "Powerful, moving, stunning!"—*The Advocate* (265924—$8.95)

☐ **PEOPLE IN TROUBLE by Sarah Schulman.** Molly and her married lover Kate are playing out their passions in a city-scape of human suffering. "Funny, street sharp, gentle, graphic, sad and angry . . . probably the first novel to focus on aids activists."—*Newsday* (265681—$9.00)

☐ **THE BOYS ON THE ROCK, by John Fox.** Sixteen-year-old Billy Connors feels lost—he's handsome, popular, and a star member of the swim team, but his secret fantasies about men have him confused and worried—until he meets Al, a twenty-year-old aspiring politician who initiates him into a new world of love and passion. Combining uncanny precision and wild humor, this is a rare and powerful first novel. (262798—$9.00)

Prices slightly higher in Canada.
